Missing My Thug & My Savage The Finale

By: Phoenixx Rose

Beautiful

"Okay, Ms. Beautiful. Everything is looking great. Your blood work came back good, vitals have checked out fine, and I'm pleased to announce that your little bun in the oven is cooking up perfectly."

"How far along am I?"

"Your baby is measuring out to be eight weeks and three days, making your due date September 28."

"The 28th? You serious?" Memmo butted in with a perplexed look on his face.

"Yeah, that's the estimated date. But as I'm sure you both know, babies are very unpredictable. They come when they're ready, so you just never know. I'll get some ultrasound pictures printed out for you while you get dressed, and you'll be all set to go."

As my nurse exited the room, I could see Memmo's face turning bright red, as if he was ready to pass out or something. I didn't want to ask because I knew the reason for his sudden change in behavior, but it would look as if I wasn't concerned at all if I didn't say anything.

"Are you okay, baby?"

"No, I'm not. November 23 is Diamond's birthday. Just hearing that was like a stab in my heart." His voice was shaky when he spoke, like he was on the verge of bursting into tears at any moment.

"I didn't even realize that. But baby, I don't mean to sound insensitive or anything, but it's coming up on three years since she's been gone."

"And I haven't shed a single tear since that day; not because I didn't care but I knew I had to be strong for everyone else around me, especially my baby. I went into full daddy mode when Diamond passed away, and I buried those emotions deep in my soul because I couldn't let Calleigh see me break down. Every single day, I've pretended that Diamond is just back in Chicago, taking care of business. I haven't accepted the fact that she's gone, so I haven't grieved her."

"I'm sorry, baby. I had no idea you were holding all of that in."

"I know Diamond is gone, and she's never coming back, but it's still a hard ass pill to swallow. Knowing that our baby is due to arrive in this world on the same day as her is like I'm being forced to finally let her go."

"At least we can celebrate both our baby and her legacy. Speaking of which, when would be a good time to tell Secret about the baby?"

"That's up to you, B. I mean, I respect Secret as my daughter's auntie, but I really don't have any obligation to her like you do. She's your best friend, so you tell her whenever you feel like the time is right."

I knew Memmo was right, but I was still scared to death of how Secret might react when the news broke about me and Memmo. Once upon a time, I cared about Diamond a lot and referred to her as my big sis. I never wanted to disrespect her in any way, but I couldn't help that I was in love with Memmo. With Secret and I still trying to rebuild our friendship, I could only hope that she'd understand where I was coming from, and this wouldn't end our friendship.

"And what about Calleigh? How do you think she's going to handle it?"

"She'll be okay. Since Diamond's been gone, she's become very attached to me, but I think she'll make a great big sister. When the time comes, I'll sit her down and talk to her about this."

"So, that means I can finally be around her, and we can be together as a family. It's not like Calleigh doesn't know me already."

"Whoa, whoa, whoa. You moving a lil' too fast, baby. I ain't trying to throw too much at my daughter at one time. Just be patient with us, aight? Everything gon' be straight in due time. But check it, I need to get back to work; you good to get home by yourself?"

"Yeah, I'll be fine."

"I'll hit you up later, aight? Love you, folks."

Memmo planted a quick kiss on my forehead before making his exit out the door. It really hurt my feelings that Memmo wouldn't let me be around Calleigh, as if I was some stranger or something. It wasn't like she didn't know me and quite frankly, all this sneaky link shit was beginning to get old. I was pregnant with his baby, and it was time he owned up to us being together for real.

Priest

"Got damn, cuz! You sure know how to pick these crazy ass bitches; I give you that."

"Oh, you think that shit funny, huh? Fuck you, T."

"Aye. Don't blame me, nigga. You the one keep dicking down these psycho, deranged ass hoes, knowing they already fucked up 'bout you. And on top of that, you decided to still marry the bitch, knowing full well she's all kinds of crazy. She ain't even the one you really wanted. I fault you for all this shit, cuz."

"Appreciate you for understanding." I rolled my eyes in Tennessee's direction. "You know, I never realized how big of an asshole you are."

"Now I'm an asshole 'cause I'm telling you the truth? Nigga, you knew you fucked up when you gave Tabatha another chance, knowing you weren't over Secret's ass. Now look what all that stubbornness got your ass — a psychotic wife, an angry baby mama, and a battery charge."

"I was trying to do was the right thing for my family, man. I thought if I gave Tabatha what she wanted, she would change."

"When are you gonna learn that you can't change crazy, cuz? I know that's your baby mama and everything, but Tabatha is a lost fucking cause. You can't cure that kind of sickness she got."

"I tried, but I'm done with her ass. All I want is my daughter and for Tabatha to stay the fuck away from me. I made a promise to myself that I would never step foot back in front of a judge and here I am, fighting another fucking bullshit ass case." Downing my shot of D'Ussé, I waved the bartender back over for another shot. Everybody who knew Tabatha, knew she had a few loose screws, and as much as I tried to brush her antics under the rug and continue to help her, all she did was prove to me that she couldn't be saved. I knew she wasn't going to take it too well when I told her I wasn't happy and I was leaving, but I didn't expect her to actually call the police and say I physically assaulted her.

When I got arrested, I was expecting to just be questioned for the little altercation we had back at the house. What I wasn't ready for, was getting down to the police station and being booked for physically attacking Tabatha. And when the detectives showed me pictures of her bloodied and bruised face, I knew just how Darnell felt on *A Thin Line Between Love and Hate* when Brandi beat her own ass up. Tabatha had a busted lip, bloodied nose, and a swollen eye, along with scratches bruises around her neck. I was flabbergasted by the fact that she would do something like this to me. But then again, nothing Tabatha did should've surprised me.

"So, what's the deal with the case, anyway?"

"My lawyer working on it as we speak. If Tabatha is willing to testify against me and press charges, I could be facing five years and up to 20K in fines. This shit is really for the birds, man."

"You couldn't be me 'cause I would have been had that bitch head knocked off."

"Aight, cool it on all the bitches, T. She's still Aaliyah's mother." Even though I could've killed Tabatha myself right about now for all the hell she was trying to cause me, I couldn't just sit here and listen to T disrespect her like that.

"Look, man, no disrespect to my lil' baby Aaliyah, but fuck

her mama. You need to get up off all that loyal shit to her just 'cause she's your baby mama, Priest. Secret your baby mama too, and she'd never pull no shit like that on you. I told your ass once before, being loyal to the wrong motherfuckers gon' come back to bite you in the ass."

As much as I wanted to knock Tennessee's ass out right now, I knew he was spitting nothing but facts. I'd always been a man of my word, and I took loyalty and respect to the heart. Those were two things I didn't play about and when it came to my family, I made a promise that I would always protect and take care of my home. But this mess Tabatha created — lying on me and throwing me in jail like I was some abusive ass nigga — was the straw that broke the camel's back. It was time I washed my hands clean from her, and as long as the good Lord allowed breath to flow through my body, Tabatha was dead in my book.

While Tennessee ordered us another round of drinks, I jetted to the bathroom to take a piss before the first round of March Madness games started. I really wasn't in the mood for no basketball game or anything else right about now. I had way too much shit on my plate to deal with — from fighting this court case to trying to make shit right with Secret. Sitting in a bar was the last thing I wanted to do, but Tennessee refused to leave me the fuck alone until I came out with him.

After I washed my hands, I was heading back to the bar when my phone buzzed in my pocket. I was hoping it would be Secret calling me back after I'd left message after message on her phone, only for her to leave a nigga on read. We hadn't seen or spoken to each other since she bailed me out of jail and things got a little heated back at her place. I knew she was only trying to avoid me because of that bitch ass nigga she called a boyfriend. She and I both knew B.K. wasn't shit compared to me, so I guess she figured if she refused to see or speak to me, what happened between us would just float in the air and disappear. But Secret should've known me by now to know, I wasn't going nowhere.

When I pulled my phone out, UNKNOWN flashed across my screen. I figured it was probably Tabatha trying to fuck with me. I didn't want to answer, but something pushed my finger to hit the green phone icon.

"Who dis?" I answered on the third ring.

"An old acquaintance from the Raq."

"Is that right?" The voice on the other end of the phone sounded oddly familiar, but I couldn't quite put my finger on it.

"Across the street in the parking lot is a black AMG with dark tints. Meet me in five minutes."

Something told me not to go, but curiosity got the best of me. Whoever it was, obviously knew me and for some strange reason, I felt like I knew who they were too, but I just couldn't grasp the voice. I thought about telling Tennessee to walk outside with me just in case it was a set up or some shit, but I wasn't worried. I ain't really have no enemies in the city besides that lil' bitch boy, B.K., and he was the least of my fucking worries.

I eased past Tennessee while he flirted with one of the bartenders and made my way outside. That nigga was already tipsy and quick to overreact in any situation, so it was best he didn't even know where I was going. I was already in trouble with the law, and I couldn't afford for his ass to throw a nigga in more troubled waters.

A black AMG was parked across the street in the parking lot, and the lights flashed as soon as I walked outside. I couldn't even front, I was anxious as fuck to know who the fuck this was and what they wanted, but I wasn't trying to walk into bullshit. My nine was cocked and loaded in the pocket of my hoodie, just in case a nigga thought shit was sweet as I cautiously walked towards the car, taking in my surroundings to see if anything looked strange. Just as I approached the car, the driver's side window slowly rolled down halfway, and my eyes locked in on a face I thought I would never see again.

"What…the…fuck?" My mouth dragged the ground as I stood frozen, looking at a fucking ghost. This shit couldn't be real.

"What's up, gang? It's been a while."

Going Crazy

Secret

It'd been going on three weeks since I'd seen or spoken to B.K. I had no idea where he was or what the fuck he was doing. Honestly, I felt so much guilt for what happened between me and Priest in the home B.K. and I shared together because the last thing I wanted to do was hurt him. Deep in my heart, I cared about B.K. tremendously, and I wanted to make things right with him; I just didn't know what to do.

On top of feeling completely overwhelmed about this whole back and forth shit between B.K. and Priest, I kept seeing and dreaming about Von. Some nights, I woke up drenched in sweat from the nightmares of the night he was killed, and then other times, I could feel his presence so strong, it was like he was watching me or something. Ever since my visit to Chicago, visiting Von's grave and seeing images of him, I felt like I was losing my mind. I knew he wasn't alive, but something very strange was happening to me, and it was freaking me the hell out.

Not having B.K. around for the moment and not even sure where our future lied, I couldn't go to him for help, and I damn sure wasn't trying to be anywhere near Priest right now. He had caused enough damn trouble for me, and even though I trusted that he would be a good listening ear, I couldn't handle him and his shenanigans at this time. The only person I trusted to help me through this was Abuela. I just needed someone who wouldn't judge me or think I'd lost my natural born mind. So,

I picked up my phone and found her name, hoping she could lighten this heavy burden weighing on me.

"Hello?" She answered on the second ring.

"Hi, Abuela? How are you?"

"Secret? Ayi, mi pequeño bebe! I miss you, sweet girl."

"Oh, I miss you, too, more than you know." I tried so hard to fight back the tears, but just hearing her voice brought on emotions that hit me like a tidal wave, and I couldn't hold them back.

"Talk to me, my sweet. What's wrong? I can hear it in your voice that something isn't right."

"Everything. I messed up everything again. I slept with Priest, and now I'm not sure if I can tell B.K. the truth."

"And what truth is that, mija? Isn't it more hurtful to be with someone you don't love? I'm sure this B.K. guy is a good man, but you know where your heart lies, baby. But you must first be truthful with yourself. Let go of the past and move on to your future."

"It's not as easy as it seems, Abuela. I really do care about B.K., and I don't want to hurt him."
"But do you love him? It's not fair to string him along if you don't love him, baby. You must be truthful to yourself, Secret. Then, tell him the truth."

"Uh, Abuela, there's something else I wanted to talk to you about." I took a deep breath, still a little on the fence about mentioning Von at all, but I needed to vent to somebody. "Please don't think I'm crazy, but ever since I went back to Chicago, I've been having these weird visions of Von. It's like he's always around me. I could have sworn I saw him on multiple occasions, but then he just disappeared into thin air. I feel like I'm losing my mind."

"Oh, mija. Baby, Von is gone, and I think the reason you're

seeing his spirit is one of two things — either you haven't let him go, or he has a message for you."

"A message? What kind of message? And why would he wait all this time if he had something he wanted me to know?"

"That's something he has to reveal to you, baby."

As Abuela and I continued our conversation, the front door crept open, and B.K. stepped inside like nothing had ever happened. But from the nasty scowl he had displayed on his face, I knew he was still pissed. He didn't mumble a single word to me. Instead, he just skated by me as if I wasn't even sitting in the room. I wrapped up my conversation with Abuela and said my good-byes before she made me promise to bring Cross back to Chicago to see her soon. I heard the shower running as I made my way down the hall to the bedroom, and I looked through the cracked door to see B.K. taking a bath.

Just as much as B.K. was pissed off with me about Priest, I was equally pissed off about the shit I was hearing about him working the streets. I wanted our relationship to work out, but one thing I wasn't about to go for was this nigga playing me like I was stupid. I'd had enough of that street shit with Von, and I couldn't handle going through it again, especially now that I had Cross to take care of. My only hope was that Priest was given some bad information, and B.K. wasn't out here trying to be the next kingpin of Atlanta, or this relationship was headed for destruction.

I stood in the doorway as he stepped out of the shower and wrapped a towel around his wet body. My eyes traveled up and down his sexy, chiseled body, and my sweet spot instantly began to moisten when I caught a glance of the thick girth hanging between his legs, making me forget for a split second that I was pissed. Sex probably should have been the last thing on my mind right about now, but when it came to B.K. and his skills in the bed, he knew how to give my body just what it needed. I didn't even realize how hard I was staring and biting my lip until his voice snapped me back to reality.

"Fuck you staring at me for?" His tone was bitter and ice cold. Barely making eye contact with me, he brushed past me, walked back into the room, and proceeded to get dressed.

"So, is this how it's going to be? You walking around, not even acknowledging me?"

"I ain't got shit to say to you."
"Well, I have plenty to say to you. For starters, where have you been?"

"Why? You don't give a fuck about me. You got the nigga you wanted, right?"

"This isn't about Priest; this is about you and me. I want to try and figure out how to make this right between us, but there are some things you and I need to discuss. So, can you stop for one second and just look at me, please?" I cautiously grabbed his arm and turned him to face me. Pain was filled in his eyes, but he tried to mask it with anger.

"What do you want from me, Secret? Huh? You want me to be okay with the fact that you running around with your ex behind my back when all I've ever done was keep it real with you?"

"Look, can you just stop talking about Priest for once and listen to me? This ain't got nothing to do with what I've already explained to you before about him. What I need to know from you is if the rumors going around are true or not."

"Rumors? What fucking rumors are you talking about?"

"About you supposedly running the streets selling drugs. Is it true?"

"Wow. So, now you're trying to turn all this shit around on me? Like I'm the one who fucked up? Really?"

"I'm not turning shit around, B.K. I want to know to truth. You've been in my life and in my son's life all this time, and if you're involved in some street shit, I need to know right now. I've been down that fucking road before, and I'm not doing that shit again. So, now is the time to cut the shit and tell me what the fuck is up."

"You know what? This shit is for the fucking birds. I ain't got time to sit here and try to explain what the fuck you should already know. So, everything your baby daddy tell you is automatically true in your book, huh? That's the way it is?"

"Stop deflecting and answer the fucking question, B.K."

"Look, I don't know who the fuck you think you raising your voice to, but you need to calm the fuck down. As long as I'm providing for my family and keeping you out of harm's way, what fucking difference does it make? I would never do anything to risk your life — or Cross's — because I love the both of y'all. Can't you see that?"

"If you love me, you'll keep it real with me. Look me in the eyes and tell me the truth. Are you working the streets or not?"

B.K. stayed silent for a second, staring me in the eyes without moving an inch. I could tell he was struggling to open up to me, but there was something else going on with him, something I couldn't really put my finger on. I felt like there was more than just him working in the streets he was keeping from me. There was something else he was hiding from me. I knew it.

Closing his eyes and breathing in deeply, he let out a long sigh before responding to my question.

"Yeah, I am. I been running shit in these streets since I was fourteen years old. But no one would ever know because of the way I carry myself. I ain't here trying to take over the world; I'm just doing what comes natural to me. I was born into the street life, but by no means am I reckless or irresponsible. I take care of what needs to be taken care of in the streets, and I when I come home, nothing else I did out there matters."

"How could you keep something like that away from me,

B.K.? You have a point that you've never brought danger to our front door, but what hurts is the fact that you kept it from me. Why?"

"Because there's certain shit you just don't need to know, Secret. I ain't keep it from you because I'm hanging out, doing dumb shit but rather, my way of protecting you from something you really ain't need to know. All it would do is make you worry, and that's something you never need to do because I'm not moving like that out there."

"That's not the point." I attempted to turn away, but he grabbed my arm, pulling me back towards him.

"Then what is it, Secret? Huh? You wanna throw our relationship away because I sell dope? That's what you wanna do?"

In my heart of hearts, I wanted to tell him it had nothing to do with him selling drugs but everything to do with the fact that I wasn't in love with him. I always hoped that I could allow myself to love him eventually, but something was keeping me from giving my heart to him. As shitty as it was to admit, I just didn't love B.K., and I couldn't convince myself that I ever would.

"I just need some space." I turned, grabbed my jacket and keys, slipped on a pair of flip flops, and left out of the room. I wasn't trying to hurt anybody — not B.K. nor Priest, but the feelings I had inside were driving me crazy. I felt like a war was going on inside of my heart, pulling me from one side to the other. Maybe I didn't need to be with either B.K. or Priest. Maybe I needed to take a step back and allow my heart to heal before I ended up hurting someone else's.

Next Level Crazy

Tabatha

Laying in bed, holding a picture of the last time Priest and I took a family portrait with our daughter, I couldn't stop the tears from rolling down my face. It was two years ago, around Christmas time and the happiest I'd ever been; I had finally gotten my family back, and that fat, man stealing bitch was completely out of the fucking picture. Now, ever since she popped back up, looking for a father for her bastard child, my life has flipped upside down. My husband had chosen her again over his own family, and I was on the verge of exploding.

The last thing I wanted to do was hurt Priest in any way or cause him grief. That man was my entire life, and I would do anything under the sun to prove to him that we belonged together, and that Secret was only trying to come between us to take advantage of Priest's heart, especially when it came to this so-called son. But when this nigga had the audacity to tell me he wanted to leave me after making love to me in the shower, I just couldn't help myself. I begged him to stay with me because I knew we could work things out, but he refused. So, he gave me no choice but to call the police on him. I would never testify against my own husband, but I just wanted him to see how badly things could get for us if he didn't leave Secret alone for good and come back home where he belonged.

Honestly speaking, if there was anybody he wanted to blame, it should've been Secret. This was all her fucking fault. Her stupid ass just couldn't stay away from my husband. Even though she claimed to not want Priest anymore and she was dating someone else, she refused to leave Priest alone. She was the reason my marriage was falling apart and why I had to throw Priest in jail. All I wanted was for Secret to drop off the face of the earth and die already, so Priest and I could go back to being the happy family we were. God knows I really didn't want to result to killing this bitch, but if she wouldn't leave willingly, she was going to force my hand. Only, she wouldn't just be thrown in jail like Priest; I was going to make sure that by the time her body would be discovered, they'd need dental records to identify her fat ass.

As so many diabolical thoughts swam through my mind, a soft knock came at my door. I quickly jumped up and wiped the tears from my eyes and placed the picture frame back on the side of my bed. I tried my best to put a smile on and brighten up my face as Aaliyah eased the door open.

"Mommy?" Her little angelic voice spoke.

"Yes, baby? Come on in."

She tipped towards me, rubbing the sleep out of her eyes. Climbing in the bed, she snuggled next to me. "Mommy, I want to see my daddy. Where is he?"

I didn't want to be the one to tell Aaliyah that her father was willing to break up our happy home for a fat ass, sloppy bitch. Well, not yet anyway. I wanted to give Priest the opportunity to get his shit together before he forced me to take extreme measures to get him to see that he couldn't just walk away from us that easily. So, in the meantime, I did what any good mother would do to protect their children's little innocent feelings. I lied.

"Baby, daddy had to leave for a few days on a business trip, but he should be back today. How about you call him and ask him what time he'll be home?" I knew the chances of Priest answering the phone were slim if I called, so I let Aaliyah call him from her phone. He could never ignore her, even if he tried.

"Okay." Taking her phone from the pocket in her robe, she scrolled until she found his number. As it rang, I whispered for her to put the phone on speaker so I could hear his voice.

"Good morning, baby girl." He answered on the second ring.

"Hey, daddy. I miss you so much. When are you coming home?"

"Daddy miss you, too baby. I love you so much, my princess."

"Can you come home now?"

"Right now, mommy and daddy got to work on some things, so I can't be at the house right now. But how about you tell your mother to get you dressed, and me and you can hang out today. Whatever you want to do, wherever you want to do, we'll do it."

"Yay! Mommy, can I go with daddy? Please?" She looked up at me with pleading eyes. I hated to be one of those parents who kept their kids from their father, but if Priest wasn't willing to have a conversation with me, then he wouldn't be able to see our daughter.

"Why don't you go ahead and get cleaned up, baby, while I talk to daddy." Taking the phone from her, Aaliyah took off running back to her room.

"Well, hello, my husband. I see you can answer Aaliyah, but I've sent multiple texts and called a hundred times and couldn't get an answer."

"I ain't got shit to say to you. Just get my daughter ready, and I'll be there in twenty minutes."

"What do you mean you have nothing to say to me, Priest? I think you should have a lot to say, actually, and it should start off with an apology."

"An apology? Bitch, you put me in jail. I knew you were

fucking crazy, but you took this shit too far. I'm done with your ass."

"You could never be done with me, Priest. I'm your wife and the mother of your child. And if you want to see our daughter, you and I need to have a conversation."

"We don't need to have shit. And what you're not about to do is play with me when it comes to my fucking daughter 'cause if you think you gon' try and keep her away from me, you ain't gon' have to lie to the police this time."

"So, you're threatening me now?"

"You should know I don't make threats. Fuck with me if you want to."

When it came to his kids, Priest had a zero tolerance for bullshit, and I knew I would be playing a very dangerous game by not allowing him to see Aaliyah. But I was willing to do anything to make him see that he needed to put our family first. Right now, he was so blinded by the lies and bullshit that dumb hoe Secret was putting in his face, he couldn't see I was the one he needed in his life — not Secret.

Nearly thirty minutes had passed when my phone rang. Priest had pulled up outside of the house and was waiting for Aaliyah to come out. I already knew there was no way he would sit down to have a conversation with me, let alone even say hello. So, before I met him outside, I called the police to make a complaint that he was harassing me.

When I opened the door, Priest was leaning against his car, waiting for me to let Aaliyah come out, but I ordered her to stay put while I attempted to get Priest to come inside. As soon as he saw me, he stared so coldly at me, I swear, if his eyes were knives, I'd be cut into a million little pieces.

"Well, hello to you too, husband."

"Bring my daughter out here so I can go, please." He spoke so curtly towards me, as if I wasn't even his wife.

"Don't you think you and I need to talk first? I mean, it's been days since you've been home. You're not answering your phone for me, and you haven't been here to check on us or nothing."

"Because your lying ass had me thrown in jail. You really think shit gonna be sweet between us after that shit you pulled? You told these people I beat the fuck out of you, and now I'm facing prison time. So, fuck no, we ain't got a damn thing to talk about. Just let my daughter come out here so I can get the fuck away from your delusional, certified, psychotic ass."

"You know what? I really don't appreciate the name calling. Furthermore, my daughter won't be going nowhere with you if you're going to treat me this way. I told you before that if you tried to leave me, you'd be sorry. I'm giving you the opportunity right now to at least allow us the chance to work this all out because I love you, and I want my family to stay together. But if you insist on making things harder, then you leave me no choice but to show you just how psychotic I can be."

"Man, look," he began walking towards me intently. I couldn't even lie, I was a little scared at what he'd do and thought about running back in the house and locking the door, but when I saw the police car turn on our block, I stood still.

"I ain't got time for your motherfucking games, aight? You want to act like a crazy bitch, I can follow suit. I'm trying my hardest to keep in mind that you're my daughter's mother, but you're making it harder by the second to not knock your fucking head off your shoulders. Now for the last motherfucking time, go get my daughter."

"Excuse me, sir? You mind stepping away from the lady?" A middle-aged black police officer approached us.

"He's not supposed to be here, officer. He just went to jail for beating the shit out of me." I began quivering and forcing fake tears to run down my face.

"You really trying to do this shit again, Tabatha? Really?" Priest's eyes turned from dark brown to fiery red when he looked back at me.

"Sir, please step away from the lady before you get yourself in trouble."

"Man, fuck that! This is my fucking house, and that crazy bitch got my baby inside and is refusing to let her come with me."

"Officer, he's been hostile with me ever since he came over. I don't feel comfortable with my child leaving with him while he's in this state."

"Listen, I'm not really sure what's going on here, but I'm going to have to ask you leave, sir. Once things have calmed down and tempers have subsided, you two can talk like civilized humans."

"I ain't leaving here without my baby. I don't give a fuck about her. I just want my kid."

"I understand completely, but if you can't produce a court order saying you have visitation rights to see the child today, I can't force her to let the child come with you. She's obviously upset and afraid right now."

"This is bullshit, man. This bitch is a fucking liar. She's mad 'cause I don't want to be with her no more, so she's doing all this stupid ass bullshit, thinking that's going to make me want her ass back."

"Look, just listen to me for a second. I been where you been before with the whole baby mama drama, but trust me when I tell you, this won't end well for you. I would hate to have to take you to jail for this shit, but more cops are going to show up, and all they'll see is a distressed woman and a hostile man. Who do you think they're going to believe?"

I could see the steam blowing from Priest's ears because he was fuming with anger right now. Grabbing both sides of his head, he paced back and forth with his eyes closed, as if he was trying to calm himself down or something. Then after a few minutes, he stopped and looked back at me, shook his head, and then got in his car to leave. I really hated to see him so upset like this, but I was equally just as hurt. All I wanted was for him to finally put that bitch Secret out of our lives for good so that we could be happy again. But if he refused to see that, then I was just going to have to teach his ass the hard way.

Beautiful

"So, how's everything going? You looked stressed the hell out."

"You have no idea. But before I get into all that, what's up with you? How's the pregnancy going?"

"So far so good. Doctor says the baby is growing perfectly, and I'm as healthy as a horse."

"That's good. Damn, B, I still can't believe your ass is pregnant, girl. What did Tennessee have to say about all of this? Is he happy? Is he being supportive?"

"Uh…more or less." I shifted my eyes away from Secret. I still hadn't figured out a way to tell her about Memmo and me, much less explain that Tennessee wasn't the real father of my baby. My relationship with Secret hadn't been the same since that big ass fight that went down after she found out Chello was sleeping with Von, and I was really trying with all my might to tread lightly around her. I didn't want to do anything to set us back again, or worse, end our friendship for good. Secret meant so much to me and now that I was pregnant, I needed her around to help me. So, telling her the truth wouldn't be good for anyone. I just hoped I could keep the truth on the low until the time was right.

"What does that mean? Is he not doing what he's supposed to be doing?" Secret stared back at me with worried eyes.

"It's a little complicated, but I'm sure we'll figure things out. But enough about me, tell me what's been going on with you. Is Priest still trying to win his family back?"

"Girl, please." She rolled her eyes as we continued our walk around the park. "It's been a lot of crazy shit going on right now, and all I want to do is run as fast as I can away from it. I'm just so tired of drama and bullshit."

"Talk to me, Secret. What's up?"

"Well, if Priest and B.K. throwing blows at each other wasn't enough mess, I ended up bailing Priest out of jail, and you wanna know the worst part?"

"Could it get any worse?"

"My stupid ass let his savvy, smooth talking ass talk my panties clean off my body, and we fucked."

"Bitch! No, you didn't!" I stopped dead in my tracks, looking at Secret with my eyes stretched wide and my mouth about to scrape the ground.

"Don't look at me like that. It was one time, and it was a fucking mistake, okay?"

"The hell it was. But then again, when it comes to a nigga like Priest, I'm sure it don't take much for any bitch's panties to come tumbling down. All it takes is one look from him to cause a tsunami."

"Uh, okay. Pipe down, baby mama."

"I'm sorry, Secret, but your baby daddy is fucking fine. The nigga walking around here looking like Black Jesus, probably having bitches orgasm when he walks by them and yet, you 'round here playing."

"And did you forget that I'm in an entire relationship, and Priest is very married?"

"Obviously, you did when you let him hit it again. Listen, I'm sorry, I know you and B.K. got a thing going on, but we both know who you really want. And when it comes to Priest, B.K.

can't hold a candle to him."

"What Priest and I had is a wrap, okay? I'm just trying to move on with my life, but it's like he won't let me be great. B.K., on the other hand, has been amazing to me and Cross. I know he loves us, and I'm not trying to hurt him."

"I get it, Secret. But you're only going to hurt him worse if you keep dragging him along when you know that's not where your heart is."

"And the most fucked up thing of all is that I'm late."

"Late? Whoa, hold up. You mean late, as in your period's late?" I stared at her intently with the feeling that I already knew what she was about to tell me.

"Yes. My period should have started five days ago, and I haven't had so much as a single fucking cramp, discharge, or anything."

"Oh shit. S-so you slept with Priest and B.K. around the same time?"

"Pretty much, yeah. I had just finished my period a day before I left for Chicago. But it could also be all this stress shit. I've just been feeling so drained and overwhelmed."

"Well, first thing's first. You need to take a pregnancy test and then go from there. And if you are pregnant…"

"Let's just pray that I'm not because I ain't trying to have another baby right now, and I damn sure don't want to cause a war between Priest and B.K. because truth be told, I don't have a clue who the father could be."

Devils and Demons

Priest

When I walked in Sidebar, the place was empty, aside from the bartender and some other dude sitting by the door, having a beer. I glanced around and noticed someone sitting at the far end of the bar dressed in all black with a hoodie pulled completely down over his or her face. When they spotted me, they waved a hand for me to come over. I approached cautiously and took a seat in the empty bar stool where I could keep an eye on the entrance and back exit. You can't be too careful nowadays with any motherfucker.

"Back from the dead, huh?"

"You know what they say; it's hard to kill a motherfucker on demon time."

"I see that. So, what you doing out here?"

"Truthfully, I'm here to make shit right. But I wanted to sit with you first just so you know how I'm coming. You and I got some ugly history, but I can't even front, I got respect for you, gang. We ain't gotta be friends or no goofy shit like that, but I just need you to know that it ain't no bad blood on my side."

"I appreciate that. And the feeling is mutual from me too. I can't help but respect you for being a man and coming to me on some real shit. The shit that happened the last time I saw you in Chicago fucked with me for a long time. I didn't want it to end like that, but you know that nigga Tennessee always on some other shit."

"Speaking of, I need you to know I'm coming for that nigga. The nigga was a half centimeter away from taking me out, and I ain't about to just let that shit slide. Ain't shit sweet over here."

I sat quietly for a minute, rubbing my hand across my chin. Nothing about this shit was going to end well for anybody. I knew from the second Von pulled up on me a week ago, he was back in Atlanta to seek revenge on Tennessee. I couldn't even blame him because if it was me, I would've probably be doing the same shit. But regardless of whatever the nigga did, Tennessee was my blood; he was damn near all I had left, and the possibility of his time winding down was starting to fuck with me heavily. I knew the type of nigga Von was, and if he wanted Tennessee dead, he wasn't stopping until he saw it through.

"I feel what you saying, Von. But why did you come to me first? And more importantly, how in the fuck are you still alive, nigga?"

"Shit, I guess heaven wasn't ready for me, gang. Doctors said when I made it to the hospital, I was dead. They brought me back, then I died again during surgery. They tell me I'm a walking miracle, but I feel like I got some work left to do, you feel me?"

"And Tennessee is the work, huh?"

"He's my number one priority. But I guess revenge ain't the only thing that kept me alive. I still got unfinished business with Secret, too."

"Oh yeah?"

"That nigga B.K.? He ain't the nigga he claim to be, and I'll be damned if he hurt Secret. She's been through too much, gang. It's time she have someone who really loves her in her corner. Folks too good of a woman for motherfuckers to keep playing with her."

"You that someone?"

"Naw. You are. What me and Secret had was good, but we

ain't meant for each other; shit too toxic."

"So what? You here to play matchmaker or some shit?"

"Something like that. But check it out, I don't want her to know I'm back for real just yet. I got to handle some other shit first before I go to her."

"Aight. So, what you want from me, then?"

"I just want you to step back when I come for Tennessee. Play time is over for that nigga. The savage from the WIIC is back." Downing his shot of Hennessy, Von stood to his feet to exit out of the back door.

"And what about Secret? When you gon' let her know the truth?" I asked.

"Sooner than later."

Watch Out

Tabatha

I sat in the Nissan Sentra I had rented for a few days, concealing my identity behind the limo's tinted windows, scoping out Secret's place. For three days in a row, I played the role of an undercover cop, watching this bitch's every move to see if Priest would show up at some point to her crib. So far, there was no sign of him, and I couldn't even deny how happy I was. Maybe Secret really didn't want Priest back anymore. Maybe she was happy with that little B.K. dude she was running around town with. I wasn't too sure, but I definitely had to keep my eyes on this bitch. I didn't trust the bitch as far as I could throw her fat ass. She wanted every fucking thing I had — my life, my kid and my husband, but I'd be damned if I let that whale have what I worked my ass off to get.

When it came to Priest, I had way too much invested in this man than Secret's dumb ass ever could. I had to go through great lengths to make sure my place in Priest's life would always be secured. And I had him right where I wanted him; everything was perfect until he met Secret. If she would have just stayed in that dried up ass relationship with Von and stayed out of my man's face, I wouldn't have been going through none of this shit. This bitch tried everything in her power to be me so she could have Priest, even going as far as having a baby, which I still didn't believe belonged to Priest. But if she thought she'd won anything, the battle was just beginning, and I could guarantee that once the smoke cleared, I would be the last bitch standing beside Priest.

After watching this bitch's house for the past hour, she finally came out with her little bastard son. I had to admit it, he was a cute little boy, even if his mama was a home-wrecking bitch. I slid down low in my seat, so she didn't recognize me as she backed out of the driveway and drove down the street. As soon as she was out of sight, I waited a couple of minutes before I exited out of my vehicle, pulling hoodie down and pushing my dark Gucci shades over my eyes. I checked my surroundings before using a pick to unlock her back door and made my way inside her house. Since I'd been watching her for a while now, I knew that around this time, she'd take her kid to his karate lesson. B.K. hadn't been around since I started my surveillance, so I wasn't worried about anyone popping up on me. But still, I didn't want to get too comfortable roaming around her place.

I scoped out her homey little pad, decorated in white and silver with specks of yellow here and there. She had a wall dedicated to a bunch of family photos from when Cross was first born, her younger pictures, and even her dead mother and sister. The bitch even had a picture of Von sitting on her bookshelf. B.K. must have been a weak ass nigga to let his woman still have pictures of her ex-boyfriend posted in their home. Dead or alive, that was a no-go for me.

For the most part, the bitch had somewhat of a cute place but nothing special. I wanted to just take a crowbar and break every fucking thing in here and use a butcher's knife to shred all of her clothes. But all of that was going to come rather sooner than later if she didn't back the fuck off Priest. Instead of wrecking this whole place, I pulled out a few spy cams and placed them all around the living room — in front of the front door, the kitchen, hallway, and in her bedroom. While I was scoping things out there, I couldn't help but notice that B.K.'s clothes were still hanging in the closet, and all of his items — like his toothbrush, shower gel, and cologne — were all still there, so clearly, they hadn't broken up. Maybe he was out of town or something.

My last stop was Cross's room, where I placed a spy cam on his dresser behind one of his little teddy bears. That was when I noticed his hairbrush with a few strands of hair in it. Using a piece of paper towel, I removed the hair, wrapped it up, and placed it in my pocket. The way I saw it, Priest would never stop pursuing Secret as long as Cross was in the picture. As much as I doubted this was his son, I figured if I proved it to him, Priest would have no choice but to walk away from this bitch for good and realize I was the only one meant for him.

Leaving out the same way I came in, I raced back to my car and jumped in before I could be spotted. I double checked my video footage to make sure my spy cams were recording perfectly before I drove off. Now, I could watch this bitch in peace and make sure my husband didn't go anywhere near her ass. Next on my list was figuring out how to submit both Cross and Priest's DNA to a lab to prove what an irresponsible, dirty skank Secret really was.

Before making my way back home, I stopped by one of my favorite bars to get a quick drink and try to come up with a way to get rid of this bitch for good without having to kill her ass. I swear, it was like God was answering my prayers because as soon as I walked inside of the bar, I spotted Chello, Secret's cousin, sitting in a booth, having a drink. And the bitch was wearing scrubs as well. Now, Chello was a crazy ass bitch I wasn't too fond of, but we shared a common interest. We both hated Secret. Maybe she could be my way of ridding this bitch out of our lives permanently.

"Well, well, I see every damn body from Chicago is migrating to the south," I said as I slid in the booth across from Chello. Honestly speaking, Chello was a very beautiful girl — chocolate skin, sexy little skinny frame with nice boobs, juicy lips, and Asian-like eyes. If I wasn't married, I would probably give her a little taste of what a bitch like me was working with.

"Shit, ain't nothing left in Chicago anymore, so I figured

why not give Atlanta a try? I hear it's popping out here. What you up to, though? My cousin still giving you hell about your old man?"

"Actually, I'm glad you brought that up because I was hoping you and I could become partners, so to speak."

"And how is that?"

"Well, for starters, I see you in scrubs, so I'm guessing you work at a hospital?"

"Hell no. I work at a fucking plasma clinic. But I'm looking for something better."

"Maybe we could help each other then." As soon as she said plasma clinic, a light bulb went off in my head. Maybe I wouldn't be able to swab out Priest's DNA, but maybe I could use someone else's. And when the results came back, Priest would be devastated and come running back to me.

"I'm listening."

"What if I paid you $1,000 to steal someone's DNA for me and submit it to a testing lab for a paternity test? Would you do it?"

"Hmm. So I see you trying to play Guess the Baby Daddy with Secret and Priest the same way that hoe Beautiful is doing?"

"Beautiful? What does she have to do with this?"

"That bitch been fucking both Memmo and Tennessee. Now she's pregnant and claiming Tennessee is the father when in reality, it's Memmo. She's just afraid to tell the truth because she knows Secret is going to dog walk her ass when she finds out."

"Whoa." I sat with my mouth wide open, frozen still by all of this tea Chello just spilled on me. First, I had no fucking idea Beautiful was even pregnant, but to be expecting a child with her so-called best friend's sister's baby daddy? Now, that's some fucked up shit. But it's the kind of fucked up shit I could capitalize on.

"So about that $1,000? Make it two, and we're in business," Chello said, snapping me out of my thoughts.

I was prepared to say yes when my phone rang. It was my next door neighbor, Mrs. Price's, nosey ass. The only time she called me was to be all up in my personal business or to try and stick her nose in someone else's. I really didn't want to answer her ass because I was trying to conduct some business, but I'd forgotten I'd left Aaliyah home by herself so I could plant my cameras in Secret's house. I couldn't afford to bring her with me and risk her spilling the beans to Priest. I had given Aaliyah strict rules to not come outside or go anywhere near the stove, so I hoped Mrs. Price wasn't calling to tell me my damn house was on fire.

"Hi, Mrs. Price. Listen, I'm not home right now bu —" Before I could finish my sentence, Mrs. Price's screams piercing through my ears sent a cold chill down my spine. I couldn't even process what she was saying because she was so hysterical. All I heard was *water*, *Aaliyah* and *ambulance*. Without saying another word, I hung up the phone and jetted out the door like a track star. My only hope was that my baby was okay.

Close Call

Secret

Pacing back and forth from one end of the bathroom to the other, I damn near burned a hole in the floor waiting for those three little minutes to tick down. I was so fucking nervous, my armpits were creating a pond, and my stomach felt like a twisted up pretzel. After I had a conversation with Beautiful the other about my period being late, I finally mustered up the nerve to buy a pregnancy test to put an end to my anxiety. Now was as good a time as any to see what was going on with my body since I was home by myself. Cross was spending time with his daddy, and B.K. hadn't been home since I told him I needed some space.

As the last seconds ticked down, I felt like I was about to pass out. The room felt like it was closing in on me, my breath quickened, and there seemed to be an imaginary drum booming in my head getting louder as I tiptoed to the sink to see the results of the test. I closed my eyes, prayed silently to myself, and begged God to please let this thing say negative. Now was not the time for me to be pregnant, especially if I wasn't sure whether Priest or B.K. got me pregnant. Life was crazy and complicated enough, and I didn't need the stress of having another baby right now.

When I saw that one line appear in the display window, I wanted to jump up and down and scream to the mountain tops. I had never been so relieved in my life because I had no idea what the hell I was going to do if there was a plus sign instead of a negative. Now, I could finally relax and focus on cleaning up the rest of the train wreck that was my life. My relationship with B.K. was still in limbo and at this point, I was ready to just cut ties and get my mind right. I did care greatly for B.K. but deep down inside, I knew my heart just wasn't in this relationship.

"Don't tell me I put another one inside you."

Priest's voice creeping up behind me scared the living daylights out of me, causing me to jump and grab ahold of my chest. I didn't even hear the front door open, let alone notice he was standing in the doorway watching me. Quickly tossing the pregnancy test in the trash, I tried my best to regroup, pretending as if I just wasn't about to shit in my pants a few minutes ago.

"Boy, fuck you," I rolled my eyes, throwing my arms over my chest.

"Shit, I'd be glad to. Cross's sleep, so I think we got some time," he replied, looking me up and down with seductive eyes and licking his luscious lips. I didn't want to react to the way he was undressing my body with his eyes, but my heart skipped a beat and my middle jumped like a frog against my panties. If I was anything like that weak ass little girl two years ago, I would've melted in his arms by now. But that smoldering look he was giving me, and the LL Cool J lip-licking wasn't going to work this time.

"Yeah, you wish. How in the hell did you even get in here?"

"I see that pregnancy test got you shook all up, huh? You was the one who texted me and said to bring Cross home because you gotta go to work and the babysitter was coming over."

"Oh shit. I forgot about that. Well, you can see yourself out because if I don't get a move on, my ass is going to be late for work." I skated past Priest, catching a whiff of his cologne. Damn, this man was something gorgeous and fine as hell. But regardless of his looks and the way I tried my hardest to mask the way I felt every single time I was in his presence, I couldn't fall for him again. I just couldn't.

Walking into my room, I proceeded to quickly get dressed for work, kicking off my jeans and sliding into my blue scrubs. Thankfully, my bag was already packed, and all I had to do was grab my lunch out of the fridge before I got written up for being tardy. I loved my job at the hospital, but sometimes the demands kicked my ass, and I hated being without Cross. As I slipped into my Nikes, I turned around to head back to the bathroom to pin up my hair when I noticed Priest standing in my doorway, gawking at me. I couldn't even front, though, the intensity in his eyes and his puckered lips turned me on just a little bit.

"Why are you still here, staring at me like you've never seen me before?"

"It's hard to tear away from something so beautiful. I can't help myself."

"Yeah, whatever. Look, Cross' s babysitter should be here any second, so could you please go? I ain't got time for your shit today."

"You the only one making it harder, baby. Front all you want, Secret, but you and I both know it's killing you to not be with me just as much as it's killing me. Even the way you standing there right now…" He glanced up and down my body, taking in my posture. "The way your breath quickens when I'm close to you, the anxiousness in your eyes, the way most of your weight is shifted to one side 'cause you're trying to keep your mind off me. I can see all of that shit 'cause I know you like a book."

"And you should also know that's bullshit. Must I remind you time and time again that I have a man?"

"Who ain't even around. Speaking of which, where is your so-called man?"

"That's none of your concern. Instead of worrying about me and mine, you got so much other shit you should be worried about, like fixing your own home and asking your punk ass cousin why he's being a dick to Beautiful about the baby."

"Baby?" Priest looked at me as if I had two heads. "The fuck you talking about?" Before I could answer him, his phone went off, causing a distraction that I was happy about. I had no idea who was on the other end of that call, but based on the shift in his attitude, something was definitely wrong.

"Is she okay?" he asked to whomever was on the receiving end, but they must not have given him the answer he wanted as his voice roared like a lion when he spoke again. "NO, FUCK THAT! IS MY FUCKING BABY ALRIGHT?!" He began pacing the floor back and forth, running his fingers through his braided hair. I could tell he was worried, scared, and pissed off all at the same time. I had no idea what was happening, but whatever it was, it couldn't have been good.

"Alright, I'm on my way now." He switched the phone off and looked up at me with complete darkness in his eyes. This wasn't Priest I was looking at anymore. In an instant, he'd turned into a fucking demon.

"What's wrong?" I was afraid to ask but was curious to know.

"I need you to do me a favor. Take my card and go grab some money out of the ATM for me, aight? The pin number is Cross's birthday." He reached into his back pocket and pulled out his wallet, handing me his bank card.

"Why? What's going on?"

"I may need you to bail me out of jail 'cause I'm about to kill this bitch." His tone was dark and evil as he turned to walk out of the door. I called out his name, but he just kept going. Luckily, Cross's babysitter, Vicky, was just pulling in, so I could go behind Priest to try and calm him down. It was obvious that psycho ass bitch was up to no fucking good and had brought poor Aaliyah into her shenanigans. Whatever she did, she'd better be somewhere praying that Priest didn't get his hands on her because she was as good as dead.

Back from the Grave

Memmo

"Daddy, I want some ice cream."

"Okay, baby. Daddy got you. But first, you gotta take a bath, and if you eat all your dinner like a big girl, daddy gonna fix you a big ass bowl of ice cream. Cool?"

"Cool."

"Aight."

Unlocking the front door to my apartment, Calleigh hit the light switch as I was locking the door. Then, out of nowhere, she screamed to the top of her lungs, as if someone was strangling her, scaring the fuck out of me. And when I turned to see what the hell had her so shook up, I damn near screamed and ran like a bitch myself.

"OH SHIT! WHAT THE FUCK?!" I yelled, grabbing my chest, trying to keep my heart from jumping out of it.

"Damn, gang, what's up? I scared you?"

"The fuck you mean, did you scare me? Bitch, you supposed to be dead." Grabbing Calleigh and pulling her next to me, I stayed with my back to the wall and my hand on the doorknob. I didn't know what the fuck was going on, but I was either about to run for the hills or pull my gun out and start busting at whoever the fuck this was posing as my dead ass brother.

"Chill out, folks. It's me, man. This your brother." He stood to his feet and removed his hoodie so I could get a better look at his face. Either this was a clone, or my baby brother wasn't dead like I thought he was for the past two years.

"Uncle Von? I thought you went to heaven like mommy," Calleigh asked. Her entire little body was shaking in fear.

"I almost did, but I got business to handle. God told me I had to come back to earth to be with you and your daddy." He kneeled down to her height and held out his arms. "You can give uncle a hug. I promise I ain't gonna hurt you, lil' folks."

Hesitant at first, Calleigh took a few steps towards Von, first touching his hands and then wrapping her little arms around his neck. Me, on the other hand, I was still stuck in a daze. I felt like I was in a fucking twilight zone or some shit. How was this shit even possible?

"What about mommy? Did God tell mommy to come back too? I miss her, uncle." Calleigh's young voice began to crack. For the most part, I was able to occupy her little mind and keep her busy, so she didn't become overly consumed with the fact that Diamond was dead, but she was a smart ass little girl who was still trying to process losing her mother. And now, with Von coming back from the dead, I had no idea how the fuck I was going to explain to Calleigh that her mommy didn't have the same luck as Von did.

"Calleigh, baby, remember when I told you mommy was an angel in heaven with God? She has wings and lives in the sky now. Mommy can't come back to earth, but her spirit is always with us, baby." I tried to comfort her, but I could see the water works about to start. I hated to see my baby cry in pain over not having her mother here anymore, but I could understand how she was feeling. Von and I lost our mama when we were young too, and the shit don't ever get easier. I tried my hardest to stay strong for my baby 'cause the last thing I wanted was for her to see me shed a tear, but the shit was still hard to deal with for me too. I was missing Diamond like crazy.

"But Uncle Von came back. Why can't mommy come back?"

"Listen, lil' folks, God had a special job for your mama to do. See, she had a gift that God needed in heaven, so that's why she couldn't come back. But I can tell you this, I saw her when I was visiting God, and she told me to tell you that she love you so much, and she see everything you doing. Even though you can't really see her, she's always around you. And right now, she need you to be a big girl and be strong 'cause daddy and Uncle Von need you to take care of us. You our lil' lady." Von's words helped calm Calleigh down, and the tears stopped momentarily. I couldn't have been more grateful. Dealing with Diamond's death and taking on the role of mommy and daddy had been hard as fuck on me. So many times, I wanted to burst into tears and just throw in the towel, but I knew Diamond was counting on me to be the best daddy I could be for Calleigh. Our daughter needed me to finally grow up and be a man.

Once we got Calleigh to relax, I fixed her a big a bowl of ice cream like I had promised her and let her get in the middle of my bed and watch T.V. Now, I could get down to the nitty gritty on how the fuck Von's ass was alive and why the fuck he was just popping up two years later.

"So, what's up, gang? You good?" Von asked, checking out the pictures I had sitting around on my coffee table.

"How the fuck you alive, bro? My mind is literally about to explode out of my fucking head right now. What the fuck is going on, for real? Is you my brother for real or some fucking clone?"

"Hell no, I ain't no clone, folks. It's really me, for real. Your lil' brother ain't dead like they wanted me, bro."

"But how? Nigga, we had a whole fucking funeral for you and everything. I helped carry your casket, and I watched them lower that motherfucker in the ground. Nigga, we threw dirt and roses on your ass, but yet, you're standing in my living room, alive and well. So, I need to know what the fuck is going on and why you waited so long to come to me." I felt myself getting angry as I stared back at my brother. No one knew the pain I carried in my heart over the past two years, coping with the loss of a sibling and the love of my life. I felt like I failed both of them because on one hand, I should have taken better care of Diamond when she was around and followed through with my plans to move her and Calleigh out of Chicago. But I got caught right back up in the streets, trying to protect my brother. And when I got the news that both of them were dead, that shit ate me alive. I'd been carrying that guilt with me ever since. But seeing Von alive, breathing, and from the looks of it, in good health, I really wanted to whoop his ass for not coming around sooner.

"Listen, bro, long story short, God wasn't ready for me yet. I still got some unfinished business to handle, starting with Tennessee."

"Tennessee? I see you still the same old Von, on that 'get back' shit."

"Yeah and no. After damn near losing my life and going through all that therapy and shit, I do have a different perspective on life. I ain't trying to be out there wilding in the streets like I was before, bro. I want different for myself. Remember how we used to write raps and shit when we were kids?"

"Hell yeah. Nigga, you thought you was Tupac, and I was Snoop," I chuckled to myself, thinking about how young and dumb we used be back in the day.

"I been thinking a lot about that shit. That's one of the reasons why I waited to tell anybody I was alive; I been working on a game plan to take this rap shit to the next level."

"Oh, I see. So, you trying to be like Priest, huh? Become a rapper and shit. Maybe the both of y'all can be the next Diddy and Jay-Z."

"You got jokes, now? I figured you would doubt me, but it's cool. I guess I gotta prove you wrong like the rest of these doubting motherfuckers."

"Aye, Von, listen, I ain't doubting you at all, bro. I'm sorry if it sounded like that, but you know you always coming up with these harebrained schemes and shit and not following through with it. But if you serious about this shit, you know I got your back. All of this shit got my mind spinning like crazy. Nigga, I can't get over the fact that you're still alive."

"I get it and I would probably react the same way. Hell, I might've even wanted to beat the fuck up outta you for keeping something like this from me, but I just needed to get my health back right and come up with a plan to make all of this shit right."

"So, what's this major plan?"

"Kill the motherfucker that tried to take me out. Once I handle that, I'm going to L.A. to get this music shit kicked off."

"And you think Priest gonna just let you come out here, stretch his cousin, and walk away free and clear?"

"That's why I went to him first. I figured I would holla at him and let him know straight up that I'm coming for that nigga, and I need him to steer clear and let me do my thing. That bitch ass nigga is the reason Wood six feet under, and I was damn near right behind him. I can't just walk away from that shit. As long as there's air in my lungs, the nigga can't live."

"Whoa, whoa, whoa. So, you went to Priest before you came to your own fucking brother? Oh, I guess the two of y'all best motherfucking friends now, huh?" I shook my head in disgust at Von. I ain't personally ever had a problem with Priest, but I knew about the bad blood that stirred up between him and Von when he started fucking with Secret. For Von and him to shake hands and wave the white flag was cool and all, but I wasn't about to hold hands and sing Kumbaya with that nigga. Priest was street nigga, a smart ass street nigga at that. Most people would say he was a man of his word and all that shit, but I wasn't buying it. We were from two different sets, and I ain't trust the nigga. Quite frankly, it baffled me how Von, of all people, could so easily turn the other cheek with a nigga like Priest. All this shit could just be an act on Priest's behalf, and I'd be damned if he played my brother like a goofy.

"Just chill, bro. I needed Priest to understand that I wasn't there on no funny, get back shit with him. The only nigga I'm concerned about is Tennessee. And before I leave this city, I'm painting it red with that nigga's blood."

It Ain't Over

B.K.

I sat in my car for at least half an hour before I decided to get out and face what was waiting for me when I walked inside my house. After that little fight with Secret where she expressed how she needed some space, I gladly gave her ass just what the fuck she wanted. For the past two weeks, I'd been renting a room downtown, but I spent most of my time trapping in the hood, racking up them Benjamins. Shit between me and Secret ain't been right since Priest found out about Cross, and it was starting to get on my fucking nerves. Yeah, maybe I should have told Secret about what I really do for a living, but there was still something deeper than just me being a drug dealer that made her so upset. But if Priest thought he could just come in and snatch my woman away from me, that pussy had another thing coming.

Finally convincing myself to go and put up a fight for the woman I love, I stepped out of the car and proceeded to walk towards the front door after hitting the lock button and setting the alarm. The house was dark and quiet when the front door crept open, and the scent of fresh linen hit my nose as I stepped inside. I could tell Secret had been cleaning and mopping by the way my 12s squeaked with every step I took on the wood floors. Coming home to a clean ass house and some food to eat was all a nigga like me needed. But with me and Secret not being on the best of terms, I doubted if she cooked anything for me. And truth be told, I wasn't sure if I would eat the shit anyway; her ass might've been trying to poison my ass or something.

As I got closer down the hall, I could hear the shower running in the bathroom, but before I made my way down there, I glanced in Cross's room and saw he was fast asleep with his little cheap ass stuffed animal his bitch ass daddy gave him. I wanted to snatch that piece of shit and rip it to shreds with my bare hands. If it were up to me, nothing that nigga bought would set foot in my house, but because I cared about Cross, I let him be. I tiptoed over to Cross's bed and planted a light kiss on his forehead before easing back out of the room. When I got closer to our room, I could hear the shower running. My first thought would have been to get undressed, join her in the shower, and fuck the attitude right up out of her. My baby meant way too much for me to just give up so easily on us. I was willing to walk through hell's fire to make sure Secret stayed with me, where she belonged.

Before going into our bedroom, I turned the spare bathroom's light on for Cross, just in case he got up in the middle of the night to use the bathroom. I didn't want him to run into anything and hurt himself, so we usually kept that light on all night for him. But as soon as I flipped the switch on, my eyes went straight to the trash can where I spotted a First Response pregnancy test box laying casually on top.

"The fuck?" I whispered to myself with a confused look on my face as I reached for the empty box. I lightly kicked the trash can to see if the actual test was inside and when I picked it up, a small piece of my heart wished that it was positive; but then again, Secret and I hadn't had sex since we were in Chicago together. Instantly, the wheels in my head began to turn rapidly. If she was pregnant, could I be the father? Or, was there a secret my Secret was keeping from me? When I turned the test over and saw that it was negative, I let out a deep sigh of relief, but my anxiousness quickly began to turn into anger. If there was even the slightest concern that she could have been pregnant, why wouldn't she tell me, unless I wasn't the only one involved in this shit?

I tried to keep my cool, but I was beginning to feel my skin heat up and my heartbeat quicken. Some shit just wasn't adding up, and I needed to know what the fuck was going on around here. Armed with the test in my hand, I patiently stood against the bathroom door, waiting for Secret to step out of the shower. A couple of minutes later, I heard the water turn off and the shower door crack open. My breath quickened and my palms started sweating as I tried with all my might not to jump to any conclusions or spazz out on Secret, but there were some things I needed her to clear up for me right now.

When she opened the door and saw me standing there, she let out a terrified scream and jumped back, throwing her hands over her chest.

"Jesus, B.K.! What the fuck?!" she spoke, her tone a little winded.

"My bad, baby. I wasn't trying to scare you," I replied, gazing up and down her semi-wet body wrapped in an oversized towel. I loved when she had her hair thrown up in a messy bun with no makeup up; she looked so angelic and beautiful. For a split second, I wanted to forget about the bullshit we were going through and grab her and make love to her right on the bathroom floor. But the way I was feeling, sex wasn't going to fix this.

"What are you doing sneaking up in here and not saying shit? And why are you just standing by the door like a damn stalker?"

"I need a reason to come up in my own crib now? This is still my home, right? I'm still paying the bills up in this motherfucker."

"Well, you ain't been around this motherfucker in I don't know how long, so I really don't know what the fuck you got going on." Dropping her towel to reveal her naked body, she ignored me as she slipped into a pair of underwear and a cami.

"You were the one who claimed you needed some space from me, so I was trying to give you that. And now, I guess I can see why you wanted to distance yourself from me. You mind explaining what the fuck this doing in the trash?" I held up the test in her face and watched her lips separate, forming an O. I knew right then and there, she wasn't counting on me finding this shit, which only plagued my confusion.

"And why are you snooping around in the trash?" She shifted her weight to one side and folded her arms across her chest.

"Naw, I think a better question is why didn't you mention any of this to me? Is there something going on that I should know about 'cause I'm not getting a good vibe from this shit. First, I catch you in our fucking home with your punk ass ex. Then, you get mad at me and claim you need space all because of what the fuck he told you. And now, a pregnancy test just pops up out of the blue? I know I ain't been up in that pussy since we were in Chicago, so you tell me what the fuck is this shit all about?"

"B.K., don't try and make this into something it's not, okay? The last time we had sex was just a few fucking weeks ago, nearly a month, and I was a few days late for my cycle. That's it, that's all. As you can see, the shit is negative."

"Hmm. And why didn't you tell me you had a pregnancy scare? Why did I have to stumble across it in the fucking guest bathroom?"

"'Cause there was nothing to tell. I took the test, I'm not pregnant, end of story."

"You know what? I really think you should stop fucking playing games with me, Secret, and tell me what the fuck is going on. Were you fucking somebody else?"

"B.K., you really need to get the fuck out of my face with all this dumb shit, okay? I just got home from a long ass day at work, and I don't have the energy to babysit your fucking insecurities." She attempted to turn away from me, which only made a nigga angrier. Before I knew it, I yanked her ass by the hair and pushed her up against the wall so forcefully, one of the mirrors hanging up fell to the floor, shattering glass everywhere.

"Stop fucking playing with like I'm some bitch ass nigga who don't see the sneaky ass shit you trying to do. You think I don't know that nigga's been roaming through my fucking house, pretending to drop off Cross but spending way more time in here than he should? I got eyes and ears all across this fucking city." Just the thought of Priest being close to Secret had me fuming. I could tell by the way she was looking at me, something else was definitely going on between them, and if she thought she was going to have me out here looking like Boo-Boo the Fool, she had me fucked up.

"I really don't give a fuck what you heard, but you better get the fuck out of my face right now." She tried to act tough, but I knew she was scared because she'd never seen me this pissed off before.

"Just answer me this. Did you fuck Priest?"

"You want the truth? Fine. Yes. You happy now? I fucked him once, but that was it."

Her words hit me so hard, I had to take a step back and really think about what the fuck she just said to me. I didn't want to believe it, but by the unapologetic look in her eyes, I knew she was telling me the truth.

"There. That's the truth. And now that you know, I think we both should just take a more permanent break from each other. I don't want to do this anymore, and I feel like I just need time to be alone."

I could see her lips moving, but I wasn't hearing the words coming out of her mouth because all I kept hearing in my head was, 'I fucked him once'. At the snap of a finger, it was like I had blacked out, and something else took over my body.

The next thing I knew, Secret and I both being on the floor. Blood was dripping from her mouth, and my hands were wrapped tightly around her neck. She was clawing at my hands, trying to pry them loose, but I wasn't budging.

"Mommy? Mommy?"

I looked back to see Cross standing in the doorway with his hands over his ears and tears running down his face. Immediately, I loosened my grip on her, and she pushed me back, scrambling away from me and running to Cross.

"It's okay, baby. Mommy's okay," she wept, holding Cross close to her. "Get the fuck out of my house now!"

I didn't even have words to say to her. It was never my intention to lay hands on Secret; I loved her way too much to ever cause her any type of hurt, especially physical. I was in no way a woman beater, but the confession of her cheating and sleeping with her ex and her audacity to try and break up with me like I did something wrong, pushed me over the edge. I didn't mean to put my hands on her, but honestly speaking, she left a nigga no choice.

"Secret, baby, I'm s —" I attempted to apologize, but she wasn't even trying to hear that shit.

"I said go now before I call the police! Get the fuck out and stay the hell away from me!"

"I'll leave. But we're not done."

Dazed and Confused

Secret

It took me quite some time to gather my bearings and calm down after what had just happened to me. My main focus was my baby, Cross, who was freaking out, crying hysterically because he didn't understand what the hell was going on. Waking up to see your mother on the floor being choked out had to have been traumatizing for him, and that was the last thing I ever wanted for my son. Hell, the last thing I would have ever expected was for B.K. to put his hands on me. Maybe I shouldn't have blurted out the fact that I actually did sleep with Priest, but his actions completely took me by surprise, and I wasn't sure how I would ever get over this shit. I'd dealt with physical abuse in the past with Von, and I'd be damned if I went through that shit again and put my son through something like this again. No way.

Once B.K. left, I quickly made sure all the doors were locked before turning my attention to Cross. I felt so helpless because I didn't know what to do or say to make him understand that I was okay. But after some time, I finally got him to quiet down and drift back off to sleep. After I laid him down in the bed, I went to the bathroom to clean the dried up blood from my mouth. But when my eyes caught a glimpse of the dark red bruises around my neck and the puffiness under my right eye that was getting bigger and redder by the minute, I lost it. I still couldn't believe B.K. hurt me like that. I understood that he was pissed about my infidelity, but I didn't deserve this.

My nerves were all over the place, and I could feel a panic attack coming on at any moment. Cross didn't really need to be around me right now because I couldn't risk him seeing me break any more than I had. The only person I could call on to come get him for me was his daddy. I knew Priest was already dealing with Aaliyah after she was rushed to the hospital yesterday, but he was the only person I trusted to keep Cross safe while I pulled myself together. The first thing on my list was to file a restraining order against B.K. and get all of his shit out of my fucking house. To be honest, as shaken up as I was, not knowing whether or not B.K. would show back up, this was probably the only time I'd invite Priest's otherwise unwanted company.

Dialing Priest's number, I paced back and forth on the floor, anxiously waiting for him to pick up.

"Yo?" He answered on the third ring.

"Uh, hey. Um, i-i-is everything okay with Aaliyah? How is she?" I tried to conceal my nerves, but it was hard not to sound as freaked out as I really was.

"She's okay. She definitely scared the shit out of me, but she's fine. Thank God for the neighbors, or else I probably would've lost my baby because of her stupid ass mama."

"What exactly happened to her?"

"Tabatha's dumb ass left her home by herself, and she fell in the pool. Luckily, the neighbor saw her struggling and got her out in time. I promise on everything I love, the bitch is dead whenever I see her ass."

"Oh my goodness. Thank God she's okay. Listen, I know you're dealing with that, and I hate to burden you with anything else, but I really need you to please come and get Cross. I just need you to keep him for a little bit."

"Why? What's up with you?"

"N-n-nothing. I-I-I just need to take care of some things."

"Don't lie to me. I can hear it in your voice; something ain't right with you."

"I can explain when you get here."

"I'm on my way."

Not even twenty minutes had passed, and Priest was knocking at my door. I braced myself for his reaction because I knew that at just one look at what B.K. had done to me, Priest was going to lose it. I didn't want him to get into any trouble or hurt B.K. because he wasn't even worth it, but knowing Priest, he wasn't going to want to hear none of that shit.

As soon as I opened the door and stepped back so Priest could come in, he glanced around before looking at me. My stomach tightened and my breath quickened as I watched his expression turn from concerned to rage.

"The fuck happened to your face?" Cupping my chin, he held my face steady while he examined my bruises.

"B.K. snapped on me. It was like he went crazy because he saw the pregnancy test I took, and things just went left."

"So, the nigga put his hands on you? Where the fuck that nigga at? And where was Cross when this shit happened?"

"I told him to leave after I threatened to call the police. Cross was asleep, but all of the commotion woke him up. He was standing at the door, watching B.K. damn near choke me to death." Reliving the physical assault from the man who claimed to love me overwhelmed me, and I couldn't stop the tears from flowing down my face.

"Come here." Pulling me closer, Priest held on to me tightly as I cried. It wasn't so much that I was saddened and hurt by B.K.'s actions; I was just getting so tired of the same old bullshit and drama. All I ever wanted was to be happy, but it seemed like every time I thought I was at a good place in my life, I got another slap in my face.

"Don't cry, Lil' One; daddy got you. I promise I'm a take care of this shit."

"No. Just let him be. You don't need to get into any more trouble."

"Let him be?" He took a step back and looked at me like I had four heads or something. "Look at your motherfucking face, Secret! That bitch ass nigga put his hands on you, in front of my son, and you want me to let him be? You got me fucked up. Whenever I see that nigga, it's on sight."

"Priest, I'm fine. He's gone now, and I'm going to file a restraining order against him. I just don't want Cross to see me like this right now."

"Secret, you should know me better than to ever think I would ever let a fuck nigga like him slide on some shit like this. It's one thing for him to hit you, but to do it in front of my son? The nigga better count his motherfucking days 'cause I'ma lay his ass down."

By the look in Priest's eyes, I knew he meant every damn word he said. I almost regretted even calling him over here because now B.K. had a price on his head, and there was no telling what Priest may do once he laid eyes on him. I wanted to feel bad for him but then again, how could I? His actions could traumatize my son for the rest of his life, and there was no forgiving in that. Hell, I may even get a lick in when Priest whooped his ass.

"Well, for now, would you mind just taking Cross? I need to think about some things and pull myself together."

"Naw, you coming back to the crib with me. I ain't leaving you here by yourself so that nigga can come by and lay hands on you again."

"No, I'm not going to your crib so that delusional ass wife of yours can bring more drama my way. No thanks."

"That really wasn't a request. Trust me, my face is the last thing Tabatha wanna see right now. Now, get your shit and let's go."

I didn't even have the energy to fight with Priest, so I just got my shit while he grabbed Cross and followed suit. He had a three-bedroom apartment downtown he claimed he kept for when things between him and Tabatha got bad. Now that she'd had his ass thrown in jail, I would guess this was his permanent spot until they resolved their issues.

Priest was nice enough to offer me his bed while he slept in the room with Cross. As hard as it was for me to admit it, it felt so good to lay in his bed and smell his scent on his pillows. It was almost like I was laying wrapped in his arms, and it made me feel so safe and secure. Priest's protective instincts were one of the things I loved so much about him. Regardless of if we were together or not, or even if he was pissed at me, he would always come to my rescue. Times like this, I missed us being together because I never had to worry about him ever raising a hand at me; he was always like my gentle beast.

Trying to take my mind off all the bullshit that had just gone down, I said a silent prayer, asking God to grant me peace and serenity as I attempted to fall asleep. Just when I was getting relaxed, something really weird woke me up. The bedroom door to Priest's room was cracked open, and I could hear a very distinct and familiar voice coming from the living room. I laid still, just for a minute, trying to determine whether or not I was dreaming, or if I was really awake because if I was, some freaky ass shit was going on right about now. As the voices continued to talk, I slipped out of bed and tiptoed as lightly as I could to the door without making a sound.

"I already owed that nigga an ass-whooping, gang. Then, the goofy wanna put hands on her? Boy, I'm on his ass, on my mama."

"It don't matter where he go; the nigga ain't safe nowhere."

"But is she aight, though? Like, how she feeling?"

"She trying to be tough about it, like it ain't no big deal, but I think, more than anything, she didn't expect him to spazz out like that. A more important question is, when you gon' come out of hiding? Don't you think Secret, of all people, deserve to know what's up?"

"I was just trying to find the right time t —" The familiar voice treaded off when he caught a glimpse of me standing with my mouth touching the floor and my eyes about to pop out of my head.

I had to be dreaming. There was no way in hell I was looking back at Von, standing in the middle of Priest's living room, looking alive as fuck. Creeping the door open, I attempted to take a step forward, but my feet were frozen. I tried to call his name, but nothing would come out of my mouth.

"What's up, Lil' Folks?"

As soon as I heard his voice and saw him smile at me, I felt my body go limp, and my eyes rolled to the back of my head. The next thing I knew, everything went pitch black.

What's Next

Secret

Two Weeks Later...

I felt so much guilt and shame in my heart for being away from my kid for the past two weeks. Since he was born, I hadn't spent more than two days away from him, but I had to get the hell out of Atlanta before I ended up killing someone. I was so angry, confused, and hurt all wrapped in one, and I knew just the sight of Priest and Von's lying, supposed to be dead ass, would cause me to snap, and both of their asses would be dead, for real this time. For the life of me, I just couldn't understand why anyone would play and relish in another person's pain and grief. Priest and Von both knew I was suffering immensely when I lost my sister, and when Von was shot right in front of me, that was a sight I had never forgotten. Watching the blood spill from his body and soak up my hands and clothes as his eyes closed for what I assumed would be the last time, fucked with my head for the last two years.

I didn't know what to think or how to feel after seeing Von alive and well when I thought I was losing my damn mind. I mean, when it all boiled down to it, of course, I was happy he wasn't dead for real. But what was really hurting me was the fact that he had been alive this whole time, fucking with my head, and when he finally did decide to pop out, he went to Priest, of all people, first. What the hell type of foolery was that? When I came to after passing out, I served Von and Priest's asses with two cold, hard ass slaps to the face before storming out of Priest's place. It just pained my soul that they could keep something like that from me, and I felt like I had no choice but to leave and straighten things out on my own.

I wanted to fly back to Chicago to see Abuela, but she had enough going on with her health than to be worried about my sick, twisted ass love life. And as much as I was trying really hard to repair my friendship with Beautiful, I really didn't trust her completely. Something was definitely going on with her ass, and I wasn't sure what it was, but eventually, I knew it would come out. At this point, no one could bail me out of my troubles — not Diamond, Beautiful, Abuela, or even Priest. I had to woman the fuck up and take back my life. I just needed a clear head and an open heart to do it.

When I left Priest's place that night, I booked a flight to Miami and locked myself up in a hotel room on the beach. Miami was the only place I could think of where no one, other than Priest, would look for me. The only other time I'd visited was with him when he had a show a couple of years ago, back when my life seemed to finally be going right for a change. I cried, threw shit, slept, wrote out my feelings on paper, ripped it up, cried some more, slept in the tub, woke up crying, ate, cried, ate some more, went clubbing by myself, drank until I had to be physically carried back to my room, and cried some more. The first three days, I cried so much. My eyes got so big, I had to peel them open. I was a complete and utter disaster.

Today was my sixteenth day of being in Miami with a hotel so damn big, I'd probably have to sell some ass to pay for it once I checked out. The swelling from my eyes had finally gone down enough for me to FaceTime with Cross. I missed him so much, it hurt to even look at his face. The only thing that brought me a little sense of peace was seeing how happy he was to be with Priest and Aaliyah. After I talked to him for a little while, Priest attempted to put his ugly ass face in the camera, and the sight of him just made me angry all over again. I had no words or energy to deal with his shit or his apologies, so I quickly ended the

FaceTime. Eventually, we would have a talk, but that time was not today.

I had made the decision to spend at least two more days in Miami, just to make sure I had enough energy and focus in me to handle my business once I got back to Atlanta. First on my list was B.K. I felt like I owed him an apology for how things took a drastic turn in our relationship and for the part I played in things ending the way they did, but as far as I was concerned, he and I were completely done. Then, I needed to work out some kinks with Beautiful. I knew that chick well enough to know when she wasn't being truthful or withholding some information. I just needed her to understand that if our relationship was ever going to get where it used to be, she needed to come clean about whatever she was keeping from me. Then, there was the matter of the dead rising again. When it came to Von, I honestly didn't know how to feel. I wanted to hate him but then again, how could I? Regardless of his reasons for coming back, I just needed to know where we were to go from here. And lastly, was Priest. Deep in my heart, I was still conflicted when it came to him because God in heaven knew that I truly did love Priest with all my heart, but I was scared that if I gave my heart back to him, he'd break it, and it'd never be repaired again. I was scared that the saying *sometimes love ain't enough*, could very well be true for us.

Priest had the type of love that you were desperate to have but scared of at the same time because it was so raw and unmatched. It was almost like finally getting a pair of expensive shoes or a piece of jewelry that you never thought you would ever be able to afford, and once you got it, you really didn't want to lose or damage it, so you become so afraid of something happening to it, you don't even want it anymore. That was the way Priest's love made me feel, and it terrified me.

I had taken a shower, threw my hair up in a messy bun, and changed out of my funky ass pajamas, into a simple sundress. The plan was to walk down to the beach and reflect on my life and the decisions I needed to make before heading back to Atlanta. Just as I was slipping my feet in my Tory Burch flip flops, a knock came at my door. I knew I hadn't ordered any room service or anything, so I wasn't sure who would be at my door. When I looked out the peephole, I spotted one of the valet guys holding a single red rose and what appeared to be a card.

"What the hell?" I said softly to myself as I unlocked the door and crept it open.

"Yes?" I asked, looking oddly at him.

"Miss Youngblood? Secret Youngblood?"

"Uh, yeah? That's me."

"A gentleman asked if I would bring this up to you, ma'am," he replied, handing me the rose and card.

"What gentleman? No one knows I'm here."

"I'm just following orders, ma'am. You have a good day."

Before I could ask him another question, he scurried down the hall, taking the stairs instead of waiting for the elevator. I, on the other hand, was left standing, looking like a damn fool, trying to figure out who in the hell knew I was here and would send me a damn rose. Flipping the card over, I immediately knew whose handwriting was on the card, asking me to come down to the hotel's bar. My mind was telling me to rip the card up and throw the rose away, but my heart was begging for me to set aside my resentment and follow through with the request.

Against my better judgement, I closed my eyes and sighed deeply as I reluctantly made my way down to the bar. I could spot Von's dreads sitting at a corner table in the back of the bar when I walked in. My stomach tightened, and I felt like my airway was constricted as I watched him, so alive and appearing to be in good health, having a drink. Just seeing him brought along so many different emotions because I went from struggling to move on from his death and facing the fact that I would never see him again to him popping back up like nothing ever happened. I was just a big ball of happy, sad, angry and confused all wrapped in one, and I think now is a pretty good idea for him to explain himself to me.

I took slow steps towards the table and when he spotted me, a big ass smile spread across his face as he stood to greet me. Part of me wanted to run into his arms and squeeze him tight, but the other part wanted to fuck him up for keeping something, like his fake death, a secret from me for all of this time.

"Damn, what's up, Lil' Folks? A nigga had to fly all the way to another state just to find you? Can I, at least, get a hug?" He held out his arms, and it took everything in me not to just run into them.

"A hug? I'm debating on whether or not to smack the fuck out of you again."

"Aw, don't do that to me, Lil' Folks. My face still stinging from the first slap you gave me. Come here, man." Grabbing my arm, he pulled me into his embrace, and I swear, it was like my body just melted in his arms. It all still felt so surreal to be standing here, having Von's arms wrapped around me and feeling the coolness of his breath brush against my skin.

"I missed you, girl."

"How could you do that shit to me, Von? I watched you take your last breath; I sat at your funeral and cried over your casket. Yet, here you are, two fucking years later. How? Why?" I tried to keep my tears at bay, but I could feel the burning sensation as the pressure began to build at the back of my eyes.

"I know and I apologize for the pain I put you through, but it wasn't all intentional, I promise. That's why I came looking for you, to explain everything, if you give me a chance."

Not wanting to hash out everything in a crowded bar, we decided to head back to my room for a little more privacy to get all of this mess straightened out. I was definitely still pissed off, but at the same time, I was anxious to hear what made him decide to pop back out after two years and what he came back for.

"So, I see a lot of shit has changed with you, ma. You done graduated college, doing what you love to do. Still as beautiful as you've always been, but I can see you've grown up a lot."

"I had to. I lost a lot in the past two years, and I really had no choice but to get my shit together — if not for me, for my son."

"Speaking of, I can't believe you're a mama now. You got a handsome lil' boy too. I guess having a baby by me wasn't what you wanted, huh?"

I could tell by the look in his eyes that he was kind of feeling some type of way about Priest being Cross's dad after I had aborted his baby. To this day, I did have regrets about terminating one pregnancy and keeping the next one all because of my own selfish reasons, but I couldn't do anything about it now.

"I was so angry with you, Von. When I found out about you and Chello, I was so fucking mad. I literally hated you and her. I felt like I was pushed over the edge, and bringing a baby into that bad blood wasn't going to be any good for you, me, or our baby. Now that I think back on it, it was selfish on my part, and I may have done it to hurt you, but I can admit my faults, and I was wrong for that."

"When I thought we were having a baby, I was so fucking happy. I was scared as shit to be a daddy, but I believed my baby was going to change my life for the better. I thought us having a baby was going to smooth all our problems out, and we would be a big ass happy family. But when your sister told me you killed my baby, I felt like I died too. I want to say I understand why you did it, but that shit hurt me bad, Lil' Folks."

"I know. I'm sorry." I could barely look at Von because the guilt was already eating me alive.

"But I'm happy you're finally happy, ma. That's all a nigga

really wanted, was to see you happy."

"I'm not though, Von. I thought I was, but I'm not. I figured that after I left Chicago and got my life together, things would start to turn around. I was dating again, and then everything started to crumble. B.K. turned out to be someone completely different, and now you're back from the dead. It's a little more than I can handle right now."

"I tried to come to you when you were in Chicago, but I really didn't know what to say to you, ma. I knew you had gone through some shit, thinking I was gone, and I wasn't trying to scare or confuse you."

"You had me thinking I was losing my fucking mind, Von. I was about to start seeing a fucking shrink because one minute, I would be looking at you and the next, you would disappear. Like who the fuck plays mind games like that?"

"My bad, ma. But a nigga still got enemies, and they still lurking. I couldn't just pop back out like Pikachu. I got to move careful in these streets before a motherfucker caught me lacking again."

"So, are you going to tell me how you survived, why you stayed away for so long, and why in the fuck did you go to Priest, of all people, first? Since when the both of y'all motherfuckers become best friends?"

"It ain't like that, Secret. The only reason I went to Priest was out of respect. My sole purpose for even going to Atlanta was for payback. That goofy ass nigga Tennessee running the streets like he some boss ass nigga, but I promise you, my face gonna be the last motherfucking thing he see before I lay his bitch ass down. I know how Priest is when it comes to loyalty and his family, and I wanted him to know that this was nothing personal towards him. I don't want him to get involved."

"And what about me? You didn't have any remorse or enough respect to tell me anything? I held you while you bled out, Von. I literally watched you take your last breath."

"I was dead though, ma. A nigga flatlined twice, but they kept working on me until they finally got me stable. I guess God wasn't ready for me yet. I had some people help me set up my funeral and all that shit 'cause that was the only way I knew Tennessee would let his guard down and eventually fumble. Now, a nigga just patiently waiting to catch this motherfucker lacking."

"All of this is so fucking crazy to me."

"Check it out, Lil' Folks." Walking towards me, Von knelt down in front of me and lifted my chin with his hand. "I'm sorry I left you and I'm sorry you had to go through all the bullshit you went through. You were my first love, and a nigga will always love you till the death of me. I know I put you through some shit, and I hope you can forgive me one day."

Feeling his touch and the way he stared into my eyes brought back so many different emotions. Maybe it was the fact that he was really alive that had me feeling this way, but all I knew was that a rush of ecstasy hit me, and I wanted Von like I'd never wanted another man before in my life. Grabbing both sides of his face, I pulled him closer to me until my lips were enclosed around his bottom lip, sucking it hungrily. God, I missed his thick, juicy lips that were so soft, it felt like I was kissing on a baby's bottom. We kissed for what felt like hours before he finally pulled himself back.

"Damn, a nigga missed the fuck out you, ma," he spoke lowly.

"I missed you too, Von. I missed you so much."

"But I ain't come here for this. I ain't come back to try and confuse you or come in between what you already got going on. This ain't what this is."

"Von, I really just want you to stop talking to me and give me what we both been missing. I just want you to fuck me. Fuck me like you used to fuck me." Standing to my feet to meet him, I kept my eyes locked on his as I hurriedly unzipped his pants.

"This ain't what I want though, ma. This ain't what neither one of us want." His mouth spoke one thing, but his eyes and quickened breaths spoke another language.

"But I don't see you stopping me. And that dick damn sure saying something different."

Be on the Look Out

Priest

"Mr. Carter, I'm happy to report that all the charges against you in the domestic assault involving Mrs. Carter have been dropped, just as I expected."

"Please don't call that crazy ass bitch *Mrs.* anything. She'll never carry my last name again."

"My apologies. However, you should know that she has posted bail but is under strict orders from the judge to stay within two thousand feet from you and Aaliyah until a court date is established. The judge will make a ruling on visitations and such. But till then, you have sole custody of your daughter, and if Mrs. C- I'm sorry, if Tabatha attempts to contact either one of you, contact the police and myself immediately."

"I got your number on standby 'cause I don't have a doubt in my mind that this bitch is going to try some slick shit."

"Unless she wants to spend the next five years in prison, she would do good to stay away."

"Man, you don't know this damn girl. That prison shit don't faze her. You can't threaten that psycho with some minor shit like that; the bitch is certifiable."

"In that case, watch your back."

"Appreciate you."

After my meeting with my lawyer, I was on high alert for Tabatha's ass. I had a bad feeling that shit between us was about to get really crazy because she simply couldn't handle rejection, especially from me. God knows I would never want to cause her any physical harm, but when it came to my life and my daughter's well-being, I'd lay any motherfucker down, including Tabatha. So, for her sake, I hoped she took heed to the judge's orders and stayed the fuck away from me.

I still had about an hour before I picked up the kids from school, so I figured I would swing by Tennessee and see what the fuck this nigga had been up to lately and hope Von ain't found his ass yet. Since Secret had snapped on me after finding out Von was alive, she ran off somewhere and left Cross with me, so me and lil' man had been bonding like crazy. I felt bad, and I understood that she felt as if I betrayed her in a sense but as long as she was safe, I was willing to give her the space she needed. I couldn't lie, I was enjoying having both of my kids under one roof, just the three of us. And in due time, I'd have my little Secret back, and my family would be complete.

Tennessee, on the other hand, I was worried about. Word on the street was that this nigga was sweeping up every damn thing. He was the man with all the money and all the drugs, taking over Atlanta, just like he said he would. While the money and being the "king of the streets" was all good and well, all that did was attract bad blood and create enemies on top of enemies. Tennessee was my blood, and I loved that nigga like he was my brother, but I had too much to live for than to get involved in his bullshit. And now that Von was back, Tennessee was in grave danger and didn't even know it. Truth be told, I had a feeling he wasn't going to make it out this time around.

Pulling up to Monaco Lounge, I parked next to Tennessee's ride before killing the engine and stepping out of my truck. Since being in Atlanta, this had quickly become one of Tennessee's number one spots to hang out. Everyone one in this bitch knew him by name, and in my opinion, that really wasn't a good thing, especially now that Von was around, lurking. If you were heavy in the streets like Tennessee, the last thing you wanted to do was create a routine where your opps could pick up on your whereabouts. And for my cousin, he was guaranteed to be at Monaco's or the strip club every Saturday night and at least three times during the week. The way this nigga moved in the streets, he was making new enemies by the day, and if he wasn't careful, he would easily get caught lacking.

Per usual, when I walked in the lounge, Tennessee was sitting at the bar, flirting with one of the bartenders. But what stopped me dead in my tracks was the person sitting next to him — my granny. Now, I was sure that anybody who's seen the dead would be scared shitless, but I always saw my granny. From the day she passed away, I'd see and hear her voice all the time. But seeing her sitting next to Tennessee with this sorrowful look on her face was nothing good. I could feel it in my soul that something bad was bound to happen if he didn't slow his roll. Even though my granny wasn't blood related to Tennessee, she treated him as if he was her own grandson, and I had a feeling she was visiting him as a warning.

As I took a step closer, she turned, looked at me, smiled softly, and vanished. I knew right then and there, I needed to holla at my cousin and let him know what was up. I had respect for Von coming to me like a man, but at the end of the day, Tennessee was my blood. I loved my cousin, and it would kill me if anything happened to him. I couldn't stop Von or change his mind for wanting to take Tennessee out, but I didn't think I could just sit back watch this shit unfold. Regardless of whatever mutual understanding me and Von had, my loyalty rested with my family. My only hope was that this nigga actually listened to me for once.

"Well, well, well, if it ain't the family man coming out to play with the big dogs. What's up, cuz?" Tennessee dapped me up as I sat on the barstool next to him.

"Shit, just chilling, fam. What you on, G?"

"You know me, I'm always chasing the bag. I'm making shit

shake out here in these streets, cuz. Aye, mamacita, get my lil' cousin a shot of Hennessy," he told the young, Spanish chick, working the counter, who smiled and obliged to his request.

"So I've heard. Word around town is you the man with the plan, snatching up all the business around here."

"I told you what I planned on doing when I got out here. You could have been on the money train with me if you wasn't so focused on chasing pussy."

"Fuck you, T. I ain't chasing no pussy; I'm just done with that street shit. A nigga got kids to live for."

"Yeah, yeah, yeah. All I'm trying to figure out is how you plan on keeping up with taking care of your family when you ain't making shit shake no more? You slowed down the with music shit, so how you gonna keep bringing in paper?"

"Money ain't ever been an issue before, and it damn sure ain't one now. I invested the money I made off the music shit. I'm still working on music but more so behind the scenes now. Plus, I got some other shit I'm working on too, so don't worry, I'm straight on the bag."

"That's what's up. I get it, you got a family to take care of, but me, I'm gon' always be a street nigga. That's all a nigga know."

"I can respect that, T, but I just want you to be careful. It's cool if you wanna be in the streets, doing what you do, but the way you be moving ain't smart. You making enemies instead of allies, cuz. And you're exposing yourself. If you gon' run the streets, run 'em, but do that shit smart, and be discreet about it instead of being a flashy, conceited motherfucker like you've always been. This ain't Chicago, cuz. You ain't got a hundred niggas behind you."

"You know, that's one thing I always hated about you, Priest. You're too fucking analytical. You always got to dissect shit and think the worst. But what you fail to realize is, when you got money and power, respect is automatic. Niggas fear what they respect, and they respect money and power. All I did was make a few moves and showed these motherfuckers how a real nigga from the Raq get down. We don't ask for shit; we take it, and these lil' niggas 'round here know a real boss when they see one, and they quickly fall in line. You think I'm worried about any nigga 'round here? I got a few hittas on my team, cuz, and you know I ain't ever running around here without a pole. I got this shit under control. Trust me."

"As always, your big head ass don't ever listen." I shook my head in disbelief at how ignorant this nigga sounded right now. But I really didn't have the energy to keep going round for round when he was as stubborn as a fucking mule. Trying to get this nigga to open his eyes and move more carefully was like beating a dead horse. The shit was getting tiresome.

"Don't worry yourself about me, lil' cuz. I'm big dog 'round this motherfucker."

"Yeah, alright, big dog. While you're out chasing the bag, piling up enemies left and right, you got one major threat lurking in the wind."

"What you mean?"

"Von. The nigga ain't dead. In fact, he's alive and well. And you, my friend, are at the top of his motherfucking hit list. I don't want to see nothing happen to you, cuz. I ain't trying to tell you how to run your life, but I need you to be more vigilant. Watch your steps." I could see the disbelief in Tennessee's eyes at the mention of Von's name. I really didn't want to be caught in the middle of this shit, but when it came down to my family, I really ain't have much of a choice. I'd be nothing short of a fuck nigga if I stood back and watched my cousin get caught lacking when I knew motherfuckers wanted his head.

"How the fuck you know the nigga alive? And even if he was, you think I'm scared of that nigga? The same way I laid his bitch ass homie Wood down and let off three slugs in that chest, I'll do it again. Von don't put fear in my fucking heart." His mouth was saying one thing, but his eyes spoke another language. Tennessee could talk all the shit he wanted, but we both knew Von was a motherfucker you didn't want to sleep on. The nigga was a fucking headache, and he didn't mind playing with sticks and doing whatever he took to get his target.

"Von came to me on some man-to-man shit and told me straight up, he want your head. You my blood, nigga, and I ain't about to just sit back and watch a motherfucker try to take you out. I just want you to fucking listen to me for once."

"Oh, so you and that dead motherfucker cool now? He felt comfortable enough to come to you and let you know he plan on taking me out? If you ask me, I think you the one scared of Von, and you want me to follow suit. How the fuck you go from being a so-called devil that everybody fears to a weak ass pussy? Let's not forget we talking about the same fuck nigga who smoked Calvin, shot your ass up, took your bitch from you, shot up your other baby mama with your seed in the truck, and you let the nigga live. Well, I got news for you, lil' cuz, Von don't strike fear in my heart, and I ain't the one to turn the other cheek like you. The same way I laid his bitch ass down before, I'll gladly do it again. And this time, he won't get back up."

It took everything in me not to ball my fist up and knock this nigga's ass out for the shit he just said to me. But when it came down to Tennessee, he was a nigga you just could never get through to. He was all about that get back shit, and that wasn't my life anymore. Shit, if I wanted Von dead, I had ample opportunity to do so. Don't get me wrong, we could never be friends, but I had to come to terms with the way I lived my life and the consequences that came along with that shit. Yeah, Von was a disrespectful motherfucker, and I'd be lying to myself if I said there were times when I dreamed about killing the motherfucker. But now, I'm over that part of my life, and if choosing to put my kids first and be a better man for them made me seem weak to Tennessee, then so be it. I ain't have shit to prove to any motherfucker.

"You know what, T? Get it however you fucking want it, cuz. I'm done trying to save your ass. I'm done having your fucking back. I still got love for you because you're my blood, and nothing will change that. But make no fucking mistake about it, if you ever come out your mouth sideways at me again, you'll be the first motherfucker to know the devil is still in me." I downed the shot of Hennessy I'd been babysitting since I sat down before standing to my feet, throwing a twenty dollar bill on the counter and walking off. It fucked me up that things between me and my cousin were starting to turn from good to bad, but you couldn't help a motherfucker who thought they couldn't be touched. As much as I wanted to, I couldn't save a nigga who didn't want to be saved.

Closing the Door

Secret

When I woke up, I was laying naked and curled up next to Von, who was snoring lightly. I wanted to say that being here with him right now felt so good, but it didn't. I felt like I was about to open that revolving door once again, running back to something familiar to mask the pain and humiliation B.K. caused me. Don't get me wrong, God knows I was beyond happy that Von was alive and well, but when I thought he was dead, I was forced to let him go for good. It wasn't easy, but I did it and last night, I allowed my emotions to get the best of me. I reverted back to that nineteen-year-old Secret, who was confused and weak as fuck.

Slowly easing out of the bed so I didn't wake Von up, I covered myself with a robe and went to the bathroom to wash up. After emptying my bladder, I brushed my teeth and ran cold water on my face. Staring back at my reflection in the mirror, disappointment spread widely across my face. What happened between me and Von never should have happened. I fought too hard to grow from the girl I was when Von and I were together, and I wasn't trying to go back down that road. I was done being that young, naïve little girl who ran to Priest when Von was hurting me, and then back to Von when I thought I could change him. In the process of running 'round and 'round like I was on a hamster's wheel, afraid to be with anybody else because the love I had for Von ran so deep, I only damaged my own heart and fucked up what could have been a new love with Priest.

Thinking back over my life since I first met Von, he was all I ever wanted because the love he gave me was all I knew. That was why it was so easy for me to keep forgiving him and going back. I didn't know anything better than him. When Priest came along, treated like a Queen, and loved me in a whole other special kind of way, it scared the shit out of me. It felt so good, it almost didn't seem right. It was a new experience for me, and I honestly didn't know how to accept it. I was so accustomed to that street love that Von gave me, I didn't know how to appreciate something different.

"Secret? Secret, where you at, ma?" Von was calling me from the bed.

"I'm in the bathroom."

A couple seconds later, I could hear him shuffling out of the bed and making his way in my direction. When he walked past me, dragging his hand across my lower back, I instantly tensed up. I wanted to just haul ass out of the bathroom, grab all of my shit, and put as much space between us as possible, but my feet were frozen still. I watched as he took a long piss, and after he flushed the toilet, I scooted to the side so he could wash his hands and brush his teeth.

"What's up with you, Lil' Folks? You good?" he asked, snapping me out of my trance.

"N-nothing. I'm good."

"Don't lie. Come here." Pulling me by the hand closer to him, he wrapped his arms around my waist. "Talk to me, ma."

"I fucked up, Von. I fucked up bad."

"What you mean? 'Cause of what happened between us last night?"

"Yes. This ain't what I want. Don't get me wrong, words can't express how happy I am that you're alive, but when I thought you died two years ago, I buried you and everything I felt for you. Your death forced me to grow up because I no longer could use you as my crutch anymore. And then you showed back up at a time in my life when I needed something familiar to fall back on. Trying to deal with B.K. and Priest at the same time was starting to overwhelm me, so having you come back was like a breath of fresh air. You've always been my go-to person, regardless of how toxic I knew you were for me; your love was what I've always known. But I can't keep going 'round and 'round in circles again." Tears began to flow down my cherry red cheeks as I allowed my truth to be shown in front of Von for the first time.

"I hear you, Lil' Folks," Von spoke, carefully wiping my tears away with the back of his hand. "And I understand how you feel. I ain't gon' lie and say I wasn't happy being with you last night, but a nigga definitely wasn't trying to cause you any more confusion. I'll always have love for you, Secret. But you're right. Our time expired a long time ago, and I won't hold you back anymore."

"I'll always love you, too Von. You have been there for me through some really great times. You taught me how to kiss, how to make love and ultimately, you helped shape me into the woman I am today. You'll always have a place in my heart."

"Ditto."

Setting Plans into Action

Tabatha

Sitting at home, looking at this bogus ass restraining order Priest put against me made me laugh a little bit. He actually thought a shitty ass piece of paper was going to keep me away from seeing my daughter or fighting for my family, but he was sadly fucking mistaken. I didn't give two shits about what a punk ass judge had to say or what the stupid ass lawyers advised against. Nothing and no one were going to stop me from getting my family back. No one.

Priest was my husband and the father of my daughter, and if he didn't come to his fucking senses, he would live to regret it every fucking day of his life. Because if he thought for one fucking second that I was going to sit by and watch him be happy with another bitch, especially Secret, he had another thing coming. We'd all die before I accepted that shit. But needless to say, I had some shit cooking that was going make him come running back home to me, where he belonged, leaving that stupid, fat ass slut alone for good.

I had already paid Chello two grand to steal someone's DNA from the clinic she worked at to present Priest with some "hard evidence" that Cross wasn't his son. Since my own husband hung on to Secret's every fucking word like a little bitch, he never once considered the possibility of Cross belonging to another man. Even though this bitch kept her pregnancy and her son a secret for a whole fucking year, Priest still never second-guessed her when she revealed that Cross was his son. Deep in my heart,

I knew that playing around with his son would rub Priest the wrong way, but if I could create doubt in his mind and cause a rift between him and Secret, I was going to rock that boat any way I could think of.

Once I got the sample from Chello, I sent the samples off, and my results had come back just in time for me to show Priest. After the little accident Aaliyah had in the pool, the evil ass judge ordered that I could only see my daughter twice a week with fucking supervision to add insult to injury. That was the most ridiculous thing I ever had to deal with in my life. I would never intentionally hurt my own kid, but I didn't expect everyone to freak out like they did. No one wanted to hear my side of the story and take into consideration that if I hadn't started taking Aaliyah for swimming lessons, she'd probably be dead. All they wanted to focus on was me leaving her home without adult supervision. Hell, it wouldn't have even surprised me if Priest called her phone to tell her to go outside and fall in the pool just to get me thrown in jail after I had him arrested. But none of that really mattered to me because sooner than later, Priest and Aaliyah were going to be right back home with me where they belonged.

Balling up the restraining order and tossing it in the trash, I grabbed my purse, along with some of Aaliyah's favorite dolls that she loved to play with, and headed out of the door. I made sure to be dressed in something really cute with a tad bit of sexy, so when Priest saw me, he wouldn't be able to take his eyes off of me. I wore my hair pulled up in a high ponytail, the way he liked it, with my favorite high waisted cargo paints and a cute, white, low-cut top, set off with a pair of Saint Laurent heels. My makeup was very light and natural looking because Priest wasn't a fan of the full face glam. I just wanted to look extra gorgeous for him today since we hadn't seen each other in weeks.

Priest made it clear to the courts that he didn't want me anywhere near his new place, and he didn't feel comfortable going to the home we once shared, so we had to meet up in a public setting that was half the distance for the both of us. What I didn't count on when I arrived at The Ice Cream Shack, was seeing Priest standing there with Aaliyah and Cross. I wanted to press my gas pedal down to the floor and drive over Cross's little body, but I would risk hurting Aaliyah and Priest in the process. I couldn't understand why he would bring his illegitimate kid when this was our time to spend as a family, and whether Priest liked it or not, Cross was not our family. But in due time, all of that was going to change, and once my husband came back home to me, he was going to have to cut ties with Cross for good.

I had to sit in the car, gather my thoughts, and try my hardest to not let my fangs show. For this to be my first time seeing my baby girl and my husband, I wanted everything to go without a hitch. I needed to make sure I made a good impression on whoever the fuck this court-appointed liaison was. Stepping outside, I made sure to secure the envelope containing the DNA results in my purse. By the end of this visit, Priest was going to be in for the shock of his life.

"Aaliayh! Hi, my sweet baby girl." I jogged towards my daughter, who was standing beside her daddy, holding his hand. She gazed up at him, searching for approval before making her way over to me.

"Hi, mommy." She spoke softy as she wrapped her little arms around my neck. My baby girl was the sweetest human on the planet. Even though everyone was trying to paint me out to be some sort of monster mother who neglected her child, Aaliyah still saw me as her mommy, who she loved.

"Oh, I missed you so much, my angel. How are you doing? Are you having fun at daddy's place?"

"Yes ma'am. I've been helping daddy with my brother. He lets me cook, and he lets me braid his hair."

"That sounds like fun. I wish mommy could be there with you guys. I miss you both so much."

The entire time, I stood there, catching up with Aaliyah, Priest never once looked my way. Here I was, barely able to hold myself up in these tall ass heels, and he couldn't even bring himself to look at me just once. To say I was hurt was an understatement. I realized that he was still upset about Aaliyah falling into the pool, but it wasn't like I intentionally wanted something bad to happen to my baby. I hated it when Priest took everything to heart and overreacted about things so small but eventually, I knew he'd get over it. And by the end of the day, I was going to make damn sure he left this place having second thoughts about his precious son.

I was only allotted two hours to spend with Aaliyah for the day. It really broke my heart that the judge would only give me such a small window to be with the child that I birthed. I was her fucking mother, I'd been with her all of her life, and I'd taken damn good care of her. One little mistake; everyone was in an uproar, and I was all of a sudden painted as this negligent monster. That shit wasn't fair at all but for now, I had no choice but to play by their stupid ass rules. Soon and very soon, all of this would be over, and my child and husband would be right back where they belonged — with me.

After my two hours had gone by and I was preparing to say my goodbyes to Aaliyah, I had to improvise on how to get the DNA results in Priest's hands. Since I couldn't get within two thousand feet of him, and this liaison was going strictly by the books, I quickly snuck the envelope inside the bag I'd brought from the house with all of Aaliyah's things in it.

"Aaliyah, baby, make sure your daddy sees the envelope inside your bag when you get in the car, okay?" I whispered in her ear, and she shook her head in agreeance.

Leaving the park, I had the biggest grin on my face because I knew once he saw those results, it was over for Secret and her fucking son. That bitch might've thought she won the battle, but I was going to be the one victorious in the end, and I was prepared to go through whatever it took to get rid of this bitch and her son, even if I had to put a little blood on my hands. If Secret didn't willingly leave my husband alone, a nice, dark, deep grave would become her final resting place. Playtime was over for this bitch.

Planting the Seeds

Tennessee

"I knew you was a freaky, nasty bitch."

Gawk. Gawk. Gawk.

"Oooh, shit. Keep sucking on that motherfucker. Make that shit wet."

Grabbing a fistful of Chello's hair, I held her head down, forcing her to swallow all of my dick. I ain't gon' lie, this bitch was a fucking pro at sucking dick. I thought my lil' Spanish bitch, Beautiful, was something special, but Chello was chart-topper. I can see why that nigga Von wouldn't leave this bitch alone. She knew what to do with that mouth.

"Damn, bitch, you gon' make a nigga bust all in your mouth." I struggled to keep my composure but the more she sucked, I could feel a big ass nut on the horizon.

"Umm, cum for me, daddy. I want to taste that nut," she replied before picking up her speed, bobbing her head up and down like a road runner.

"Ahh, shit! I'm about to nut! Ahhh, shiiiiitt!" This bitch had me hollering like a bitch as she sucked the nut right out of me. Even after I came, she still wouldn't stop sucking. Chello had a mouth like a fucking vacuum, sucking up every single drop.

"Damn, bae. That was some good shit." My breathing was winded as I laid back on the bed, trying to catch my breath.

"I'm glad you enjoyed it, daddy. So, you got my money or

what?" Getting off her knees, she made her way to the bathroom to rinse her mouth out.

Chello had rolled up on me earlier while I was at the lounge, talking about she had some juicy news to tell me, something I probably wouldn't be too happy about. A nigga was already feeling some type of way about getting into it with Priest's ass, and I really wasn't trying to hear whatever the fuck she had to say. Chello was always a messy ass, jealous bitch, and a nigga ain't have time for that bullshit right now but since Von's dead ass was supposedly not dead after all, and was planning revenge, I figured I would hear her ass out.

All this time, I thought she was rolling up to holla at me about Von being back around but in reality, this bitch hit me with some news I never would have expected. That slimy, goofy ass hoe, Beautiful, had apparently been playing on my motherfucking top and was fucking Memmo behind a nigga's back. And to add cherries on top, he was the nigga that got her pregnant and not me, which explained why she'd acted so fucking distant from me when she found out she was pregnant. When it all boiled down to it, I really didn't give two fucks about being a baby's daddy. That was Priest who was on that family man shit. I wasn't ready for that type of responsibility anyway, so it really didn't matter who the little bastard belonged to. But what I didn't appreciate was this bitch playing with me, knowing damn well there was bad blood between me and that nigga Memmo. Shit, this bitch could have been plotting against me, trying to set me up this whole fucking time for that nigga to get some get back.

So, after finding out this new information, a nigga was hotter than fish grease and ready to run down on both Beautiful and Memmo's bitch ass. But I needed to move carefully. As much as I hated to admit it, Priest was right about one thing — a nigga was catching some backlash from shutting down all these bum ass niggas' trap houses. After I successfully snatched up B.K.'s supplier, I was the nigga in these streets. I was distributing the best products at lower costs, which shut down all the local trap houses. And let's just say, niggas around here were in their chest about that shit. B.K., and along with some other niggas, had sent me a few threatening messages, but I was never worried because I kept that pole next to me, and I had a few hitters riding alongside me too. One thing a nigga could never take away from me was my heart. I was a motherfucking soldier, and fear was one thing I never had. But I was no dummy either. If Von was really alive and lurking for me like Priest said, I damn sure needed to watch my fucking back and move with caution.

Me and Chello ended up getting wasted at the lounge, which led us back to a hotel room. For double the price of what she wanted for her little information, she gave a nigga sloppy top. I ain't really want the pussy, and after she sucked me off the way she did, I didn't have the energy to fuck her if I wanted to. I threw a couple stacks on the bed for her and adjusted my clothes before making my way out of the room. Heading to my car, I tried to come up with a master plan to get this bitch Beautiful and Memmo for trying to sneak one up on me. Ain't no way I would let that hoe slide like I was some goofy ass nigga. But as I approached my car, some weird shit caught my eye. All four of my fucking tires had been slashed, and my windshield was busted.

"Motherfucker! Who the fuck stupid enough to fuck with my shit?!" I yelled out to myself. Fuming at the mouth, I could feel my blood pressure rising, and all I saw was red. As I stood in front of my car, examining the damage, I heard footsteps quickly approaching me, but before I had the chance to reach for my gun, I heard the sound of whoever was behind me cock their gun. The cold steel was pressed firmly against the back of my head, and I could feel their breath on my neck.

"I wouldn't do that shit if I was you, nigga, unless you ready to meet your maker," B.K.'s voice spoke in a low tone.

"You ain't got the balls to approach me like a man so

instead, you sneak up behind me like a bitch."

"Yeah, nigga. Just like you wasn't man enough to step to me face-to-face and take my business away. You crept behind my back like the snake ass bitch nigga you are. Nigga, did you really think I was going to let you get away with that shit?"

"I mean, what can you really do about it? Kill me? Nigga, I can't help it that I was able to come to your city and take over this shit. That's on you, playboy."

"After I put you on game, bitch! You wouldn't have no fucking connects or none of that shit if it wasn't for me, you goofy ass nigga. Shit, all you had to do was say you wanted to step out and run your own shit. But you don't know shit about loyalty, do you?"

"I'm loyal to the only motherfucker that matters and that's me, nigga. As long as I get on top, I really don't give two fucks about who I gotta step on to get there. If that hurts your feelings, oh fucking well. It is what the fuck it is, nigga. So, what you wanna do? Shoot me? Do whatever you gotta do 'cause that gun to my head ain't scaring me."

"Nawl, I ain't gonna kill you, Tennessee. But I am gonna leave you with a message, one for you and your fuck ass cousin."

Next thing I knew, something hard forcefully hit me in the back of the head, knocking me down to the ground, followed by some swift kicks to my stomach, back, and rib cage. If a nigga wanted to fight back, I couldn't because I was seeing stars after that blow to the back of my head. All I knew was this nigga was beating the fuck out of me, and I couldn't do a damn thing about it but take this ass whooping.

After getting the shit kicked out of me for what felt like hours, B.K. finally let up off me. Blood poured from my mouth and nose, and it felt like my entire rib cage was broken. My eyes had begun to swell so big, I could hardly see out of them. This nigga had beat my ass damn near unconscious. Kneeling down in front of me, he squeezed my cheeks together till they were touching each other on the inside.

"I would advise you to get the fuck out of my city, bitch. Or the next time, a good ass whooping won't be the only thing I give your goofy ass. And tell your bitch ass cousin to stay the fuck away from my woman, or he's gonna receive the same fucking treatment." Taking the butt of his gun, B.K. whacked me in the face twice before spitting on me.

I tried to get up, but my whole body felt broken. My head was spinning like I was going sixty miles a second on a merry-go-round, and my vision got blurry until everything just went black. I didn't know if I was dying or what, but all I did know was that a nigga needed help, bad.

<h1 style="text-align:center">On Yo' Ass</h1>

Von

"So, what happened? You got your girl back or some?"

"Naw, it wasn't nothing like that. Me and Secret over, bro."

"Nigga, stop lying. You ain't go all the way to Miami for nothing. I know y'all fucked."

"I mean, yeah, we fucked but only because emotions were running all over the place. Shit, it's been over two years since we had seen each other, so it was bound to happen. But getting back together is out of the window. I got love for Secret, and always will, but we better off without each other."

"Damn, lil' bro, you really done changed. I remember you used to be ready to light up the whole motherfucking city about Secret's ass. You said you would never let her go. But now look at how you done gave up on your woman so easily. You do know, she just gon' run right back to that nigga Priest, right?"

"It is what it is, bro. That was the old me, though. I was on that toxic shit, feeling untouchable, like Secret would never leave me. Truth be told, she deserve better than me, and maybe Priest is the better man."

Memmo snapped his head in my direction with a dumbfounded look on his face. I knew he was probably thinking I had lost my fucking mind and to be honest, it was kind of hard admitting to myself that Priest was a better man for Secret than I was. It damn sure wasn't something I would have ever imagined hearing myself say, but it was the truth. It took me some time to realize and accept it, but my relationship with Secret had more bad times than it did good. Even though those good times were the very best times of my life, the bad shit just took over. An infinite number of 'I'm sorrys' and a lifetime of making it up to her still wouldn't be enough to repair all the damages I caused. It hurt like hell to finally accept it and let her go, but the love and respect I had for her helped me to overcome.

"Nigga, is you tweaking? You died and came back a whole different type of nigga or some? 'Cause this ain't my lil' brother sitting next to me right now saying all this stupid shit."

"I'm still the same Von; don't get that shit twisted. I'm just not that wild lil' nigga no more, bro. I'm grown now, and all that bullshit me and Secret been through is over with. Trust me, my love for her will always run deep, but that relationship shit ain't what it is anymore."

"So, you're willing to see the woman you loved and was willing to die for, be with the same motherfucker you was going to war with? I don't give a fuck what you say, that shit sound stupid as fuck."

"Man, whatever. It is what it is. You can get off my dick right now and tell me what the fuck been going on with you. What's Atlanta been like?"

"Shit, you know I been adapted to this shit long before the rest of these motherfuckers decided to pop up here. Atlanta too fucking small for all of us Chicago niggas, bro.

"You ain't lying. I know the word gonna get out about me being here sooner or later, but I ain't trying to hide no more. I want motherfuckers to know I'm back. You know I ain't ever been the type of motherfucker to hide; I want these niggas to see how I'm coming."

"Tennessee still at the top of the list?"

"You damn straight. You think I'm a let this nigga keep breathing like he ain't try to take my motherfucking life from me? Fuck that. Niggas gotta die, and it ain't gon' be me."

"I hear you, bro. And you already know how I'm coming behind you, all gas and no motherfucking breaks."

"Nah, bro, this is all on me. I appreciate you for always having my back and looking out for me as a big brother, but this my mess to deal with. And besides, you got my lil' niece to be here for. She already lost her mother, bro. She can't afford to lose you too, especially behind my mess."

"But Von, you don't know how Tennessee is coming and how many niggas he got coming behind him. Shit, last I heard, he and B.K. were doing business together. The nigga could have all kind of allies out here, bro. We ain't in Chicago no more, and you ain't got Wood on the side of you no more. Remember that."

"Thanks for the reminder." I glanced down at the portrait of my best friend I had tattooed on the inside of my arm. Wood was one of my closest friends I ever had; shit, truth be told, we were closer than I was with my own blood brother. And that fuck nigga, Tennessee, is the reason my nigga was six feet under. But make no mistake about it; I was going to get my lick back.

"Von, I'm serious. Just move carefully and watch your motherfucking back out here. Don't get caught lacking."

"The nigga may have caught me once, but I'll be damned if the nigga think he finna take me out for real this time. This shit ain't sweet over here."

"Just be smart about this shit. I can't afford to lose you for a second time, not before you meet your new niece or nephew."

"Say what? Who the fuck you knocked up 'round here?"

"It's a long ass story, bro, but me and Beautiful started fucking around a lil' while ago, and now she's pregnant."

"Beautiful?" I shot that nigga a dirty ass look. That bitch never been my cup of tea. Her hating ass always had some slick shit to say about me and Secret's relationship, and she was the reason Secret found out about me and Chello. I couldn't stand that long nose, big ear having ass hoe.

"Nigga, you fucking Beautiful? Out of all the pretty ass pussy running 'round here, you smashing that bitch?"

"Honestly, I was just using her dumb ass to give me all the dirt she could on Tennessee's ass. Shit, I was planning my own get back on that nigga, and I heard she was supposedly fucking around with him too, so I just used her as an opportunity to get him."

"And you think you can trust that hoe?"

"Hell nah. I know that bitch probably playing both sides. I was gon' knock her ass off once I got his bitch ass anyway, but if she really pregnant with my kid, I don't know what I'm going to do. She really thinking we about to be a real couple out here, but I could never cuff that hoe."

"Before you cut her ass off, see if she found out anything on Tennessee's ass. He's next on my list, after I handle B.K.'s bitch ass."

"I told that nigga it wasn't a smart move for him to get romantic with Secret. Nigga supposed to be your homie, and he backdoor your ass as soon as he think you're dead."

"I didn't mind him keeping a close watch on her to make sure nobody fucked with her, but this nigga went and jumped in a whole relationship like that shit is sweet. I got something for his bitch ass too."

"I think the nigga been trying too fucking hard to be like you anyway. He wanna act like he running shit 'round here and then trying to go to war with Priest. I tried to warn his ass, he better know what the fuck he doing if he try to step down on Priest. That ain't the nigga he want smoke with."

"Priest might get on his ass, but I'm worse."

"You just evil, Von. It's like you turn into a demon seed

when it comes to Secret's ass."

"You damn right. I'm the demon that's about to introduce B.K. to hell on earth. He gon' learn. I'm not the fucking one to cross."

Too Late to Apologize

B.K.

After a million failed attempts to call and text Secret to make up for the way I acted the last time we saw each other, she left me no choice but to pop up on her ass. I wasn't just some lame ass motherfucker willing to walk away from her without another word. Shit, if we were going to be honest with each other, she was the reason I acted the way I did. She was the one who let that goofy motherfucker Priest fill her head with a bunch of bullshit and fuck up what we had. I loved Secret too much to give up on us so easily, and I damn sure wasn't about to sit back and let her punk ass baby daddy snake his way back to her. Ain't no way.

I knew it was risk pulling up to the crib unannounced, but it was a risk I was willing to take. She refused to answer the phone when I called, so she left a nigga no other choice but to pop up. I was dead ass wrong for putting my hands on her, but she was just as guilty for provoking me with that slick ass mouth of hers. But regardless of whatever she said to me, I should have been a man about my shit. She didn't deserve for me to lay hands on her, and I was gonna make sure I did whatever I needed to do, so she could understand how sorry I was, and that I'd do anything to keep us together. I wasn't ready to just walk away.

Walking up to the front door, the smell of Mexican food filled my nostrils, and I could hear SWV's "Weak" playing. I twisted the knob, but it was locked. She hadn't changed the locks on me, and that was a good thing because I still had my key.

Unlocking the door, I cautiously stepped inside, praying that I wasn't about walk up on her getting dicked down by Priest. Making my way around the corner to the kitchen, I spotted my baby swaying her curvy ass hips from side to side as she danced to the beat. She was wearing a sexy ass dress with a deep slit on the side that almost reached her hip, and it hugged her body like a glove. I leaned against the wall and enjoyed the view while she stirred some fajitas on the stove and sang along with the song. A gentle smile spread across my face, watching her body move so fluidly, and all I could think about was grabbing her in my arms and making love to her right on the kitchen table. My mind was so deep in thought with all the things I wanted to do to her, when she finally turned around to notice me, her yelp scared the shit out of me.

"Ahh! Jesus Christ!" she yelled out, grabbing her chest in a petrified manner. "What in the entire fuck, B.K.? Are you crazy?"

"I'm sorry, sweetheart. You looked like you were having a good time, and I didn't want to disrupt you. In fact, I was enjoying the view."

"How did you even get in here? People lock their doors for a fucking reason."

"Last I checked, this was still my house too. I only came over here because you weren't answering my calls or texts, and I think you and I need to have a conversation."

"No, we don't need to have shit. I'm done. What you need to do is get the fuck up outta here, B.K. There is nothing for us to discuss." She attempted to stomp past me, but I blocked her path. If she thought I was just going to let her escape that easily, she had another thing coming.

"Don't walk away from me when I'm trying to talk to you. The least you could do is hear me out, baby."

"Do not call me 'baby'. You put your fucking hands on me in front of my son, and you think you can just waltz back in here like everything is all peaches and cream? Nigga, you got me fucked up. You lucky I don't call his daddy to come beat your punk ass."

"Wow. So it's like that? You wanna call your punk ass baby daddy to try and step down on me? See, I came over here to have a grown up conversation with you and apologize for putting my hands on you, but I see you still want to talk greasy to me. All that disrespectful shit you be doing and saying to me ain't gon' fly, Secret. You gonna fuck around and get you and your bitch ass baby daddy fucked up."

"Boy, please. I ain't worried about you, okay? And trust and believe, if you knew like I knew, you'd watch your fucking back 'cause Priest is looking for you, and when he finds you, he's definitely gonna tax that ass. So why don't you do yourself a favor and please get the fuck up out of my house. You and I are over. Done. And I don't ever want to see or hear from your weak, punk ass again."

"Nah, you're sadly mistaken, sweetheart. Ain't shit over until I say it's over." Grabbing her by the forearm, I pushed her up against the wall, keeping a tight grip on her. "You really think a nigga about to let you just walk away? You got me fucked up. I love you, Secret, and I want us to be a family again. I ain't going nowhere and you damn sure ain't going nowhere. So, why don't we save ourselves the dramatics and let's just kiss and makeup."

"B.K., you need to get the fuck off me and get out of my house before I call the police. I'm not playing with you." She struggled to loosen herself from me, but the more she pulled, the tighter I held on to her.

"So what? You think you just about to leave me and go back to that goofy ass nigga? Huh? You think I'm just gonna let you leave me like some lame ass motherfucker? Bitch, you belong to me. You hear me?" Her rejection was bringing out a rage in me that I tried to conceal, but the more she talked reckless to me, the angrier I became. When I was a kid, I watched my dad beat up on every woman he had. I used to swear to myself that I would never put my hands on a female but somehow, I knew that abuse he instilled in me would always be there. I fought like hell to keep it from ever showing, but every time a bitch got slick at the mouth and disrespected me, it made it harder to just turn the other cheek.

"B.K., get the fuck off me! Just stop it!"

"Fuck that! You not about to leave me, baby. I love you and I need you. We can work through this, baby, I know we can. I just need you to trust me."

Out of nowhere, someone yanked on the back of my shirt, pulling me with force away from Secret and when I turned around, I swear, I thought my eyes were going to pop out of my head as I stared back at a fucking ghost. Ain't no fucking way I was looking into the eyes of Von 'cause if memory served me correct, the nigga had been dead for two fucking years. I didn't have a chance to say or do shit because before I could wrap my head around what the fuck was going on, the nigga had struck me so fucking hard with a left hook, it felt like my soul left my body.

I'd be lying if I said I wasn't freaking the fuck out, which was probably why this nigga was beating the fuck out of me like a lil' kid getting his ass whipped by his daddy. I was trying my damnedest to fight his ass back, but the lil' nigga was too fucking quick, and every blow was vicious. Now I knew just how that nigga felt on that movie, *Four Brothers*, when Bobby was beating the fuck out of a nigga's ass with a brick 'cause that's just how hard Von's fists connected with my face. Next thing I knew, we were outside, and all I could hear was Secret yelling for Von to stop. I was glad as fuck that she was trying to break this shit up 'cause a nigga couldn't take it anymore.

"Get yo' bitch ass up outta here, nigga. You lucky I don't stretch your fuck ass right here and now, bitch boy. Don't ever put your fucking hands on her again, goofy ass nigga."

"It's good, Von. It's over. Just leave him alone."

As I tried to find my balance and stop my head from spinning like I had just gotten off a merry-go round, I could hear Von still fussing in the distance, followed by a loud screeching noise like someone had just slammed on their brakes really hard. Then, out of nowhere, a gun started going off, and I could hear Secret screaming.

"Secret, get back! Get down!"

Before I could register what was happening, I felt a sharp pain hit me in the back and in the leg. My body went limp as I hit the pavement, and everything around me began to slow down, like everything was moving in super slow motion. Loud screams went faint, and it was getting harder for me to breathe by the second. I felt like I was under water, and my lungs were getting too full for me the breathe properly. Then, everything just stopped and went pitch black.

Nice Try

Priest

"You sure you okay?"

"I'm fine. Just a little shaken up. I'm so tired of watching people die right in front of me. The shit is traumatizing, man."

"I can't say I know how you feel, but you know I'm here for you, right?"

"Yeah, but that don't stop the nightmares, thanks to your dumb ass cousin. B.K. was a fucking idiot, but he didn't deserve to be gunned down like some animal. You need to do something about him, Priest. Tennessee is fucking crazy."

"Don't worry about Tennessee. I'm gonna take care of it."

"What if Cross was home? What if he would have hit me instead of B.K.?"

"He better be thanking God my son wasn't here, and not one of those bullets even grazed you, or I would have killed his ass my damn self. Tennessee is just irrational and reckless. He don't fucking think shit through before he react."

"This shit is just so crazy how quick things can happen. One minute, B.K. is standing in my kitchen, trying to force us to get back together and within ten minutes, he's dead. I just wanted him to understand that we were over, but I would have never wished death on him. This is beginning to be too fucking much for me, and I feel like I'm about to explode. I'm glad Von popped up when he did and pushed my ass out of the way. Or there ain't no telling how this would have turned out. I could be

"

laying right next to B.K."

"The nigga damn sure knows the right time to show up. Where did he go, anyways?"

"I don't even know. He just told me to get in the house and he took off running. My guess is he went looking for Tennessee."

I could tell Secret was trying to hold it together but at any given second, she would break. I hated to see her like this and wanted nothing more than to just take away the pain that she was feeling. The savage in me wanted to say fuck that nigga, and he'd better be glad Von and Tennessee got to his bitch ass before I did, but I wasn't trying to sound like a heartless motherfucker when Secret was already hurting.

"I'm right here for you, Secret. You know I got you, baby." I wrapped my arm around her, placing a gentle kiss on her forehead.

"Can we just change the subject, please? Let's talk about you being super daddy, taking on both kids at once. How was Cross?"

"Come on now, baby. I'm Superman. I know how to take care of my kids. Aaliyah helped me out a lot with Cross; that's my lil' lady."

"He didn't cry for me or nothing? I missed him so much."

"He had his moments, but daddy took care of that. Daddy gon' take care of his family and make sure his kids straight. And make sure my baby straight too." I snuck another kiss on Secret's cheek before she pushed me away.

"Stop playing with me, Priest."

"The only one playing is you, Lil' One. You gon' be mine again, trust me."

"Whatever." She rolled her eyes at me. "Anyway, let me get going before that psycho bat pulls up. I wouldn't want her thinking I'm trying to impose on her time with Aaliyah 'cause I don't have the time or energy to play with her ass today."

"Hold up a minute. I wanted to holla at you about something before you leave, so you ain't sidetracked by anything."

"What's up?"

I pulled out the fake ass DNA test Tabatha had rigged up, snuck it into Aaliyah's bag, and handed it to Secret. I already mentally prepared myself for her to snap on my ass for what I was about to reveal to her, but it was better that I let her know what I did before Tabatha's big ass mouth came around, being shady.

"What the fuck is this?"

"This is the bullshit Tabatha tried to cook up. She been saying from day one Cross ain't my son and I should get a DNA test. So, she had this bullshit made up, like it would put any doubt in my mind."

"But Priest, how did she even get DNA from my son to test him?"

"I don't think she did, Secret. She probably found somebody to help her rig this shit up. I don't know how the crazy bitch did this shit, but I know it's all fucked up."

"And this is the bitch you decided to marry? A crazy, delusional ass bitch. Who the fuck would stoop this low to do some dumb shit like that? Hell, if you wanted a DNA test for Cross, I would have gladly given it to you."

"But that's the other thing I wanted to tell you. The reason I called this bullshit was because I already had a DNA test done for Cross." I couldn't front, I was a tad bit nervous admitting the truth to Secret 'cause I just knew she was going to knock my head off, but my intentions were never malicious or to hurt her.

"You did what?" She glared at me with a disgruntled look on her face. "What, you didn't believe me or something? You really think I would try and pin a baby on you?"

"No, it wasn't like that. I just needed to know for myself. You were still messing around with Von, and I didn't know about my son until a whole year later. I trusted what you told me, but I just needed to be sure for myself."

"I'm not mad, Priest, but you could have said something to me about this. I would have given you a test if that what was you wanted. I understand your reasons for wanting to be sure, but we could have talked about it together, though."

"You right and I apologize. Can we kiss and make up?" I pretended like I was about to kiss her, but she mushed the fuck out of my ass.

"I don't think so."

"Stop acting like you don't want a nigga back. You know what time it is."

"Bye, Priest. Don't nobody want your ass but that fatal attraction wife of yours."

Fight Night

Secret

"Damn, look at you, Miss Mamas. That baby is putting weight on your ass already, I see."

"Girl, tell me about it. I'm just getting into my second trimester, and I feel like a fat ass pig. None of my clothes fit me anymore."

"But you do look amazing. Your face is glowing. How are you feeling?"

"I feel pretty good. But the real question is, how are you feeling? I heard about what happened to B.K. I'm so sorry for your loss."

"Thanks, but it really wasn't my loss. I mean, I didn't want to see him get murdered right in front of me, but I had a feeling that he wasn't going to make my life any easier after I told him it was over. I guess I have your baby daddy to thank for putting B.K. out of his misery."

"Girl, I don't even want to mention that nigga's name. I thought Tennessee would be something different but obviously, he's not. He is completely unstable these days, and I do not trust him. We haven't seen or spoken to each other in weeks, and I don't plan on talking to his ass anytime soon."

"He could have fucking killed me and my son if he was home. I'm just so grateful Von was there to push me out of harm's way." As soon as I mentioned Von's name, the water Beautiful was drinking shot out of her mouth like some sprinklers had gone off. Water splashed all over the table we were sitting at, and it was like the entire restaurant stopped, and everyone was staring at us.

"Damn, B, can you display a little decorum? You got all these folks looking at us like we're stupid." I rolled my eyes at her, wiping off the water and saliva mixture from the table.

"A little decorum? Bitch, you just said Von's name. Are you sure you didn't get hit with a stray bullet and your memory is shaken or something? 'Cause, baby, Von is dead, unless you found a new nigga named Von."

"I'm afraid not. Rayvon Dowers is alive and well. And believe me, I was just as freaked out as you are right now."

"How the fuck is that even possible, Secret? Von has been dead for damn near three years. Tennessee killed his ass."

"Shit, that's what we all thought. I'm the one who witnessed his ass get shot. Apparently, he was dead, but the doctors worked on him until they revived him. Now, he's back."

"What in the True to the Game, Quadir Richards, back from the dead type shit is this?"

"Who you telling? The shit still freaks me out."

"Sooo, does this mean y'all are going to give it another go? I mean, he came back to find you, and he saved you from Tennessee's rampage."

"No. Von and I have reached the end of the road in our relationship. I'll always love and care for him, but that's done."

"Damn, Secret, I thought we were about to endure another go around of Priest and Von going to war over you. I don't think this city would be able to handle that."

"No, girl, I've just come to the conclusion that I need to take a fucking break from men, period. Obviously, I keep picking the wrong motherfuckers to date, and the shit never ends well. First Von with all his bullshit, to Priest being more than I can handle, and now B.K. turning out to be someone completely different from the man I first met. It's just too fucking much, and I'm over this love shit."

"No, see, it's the fact that you want that type of love Priest gave to you, but you're afraid to let him back in. So, you're trying to recreate that love in another human being. That shit is not gonna work, baby. I'm sorry."

"First of all, this ain't *Iyanla: Fix My Life*, okay? If I wanted Priest, I could have his ass. That's not what I want anymore either."

"Secret Youngblood, you forget who you're talking to. Girl, I know you like the back of my hand. You can sit and front like you're over Priest, but I can see it in your eyes; that's a lie. I know what you had with Von was something like *CrazySexyCool*, but the shit was toxic. He made you happy but equally sad at the same time. But when it comes to Priest, that's a whole 'nother bracket. That's a man who knows how to love and respect women. I saw you happy with Von, but when you were with Priest, it was a different type of happiness. Priest brought peace and serenity to your life after Von filled it with pain and chaos. You can talk all the shit you want, but you still love that man, and you know it."

"Well, well, well. If it ain't my two besties. What's up, gang?"

Before I could respond to Beautiful's nonsense logic on my feelings for Priest, Chello's hoe ass interrupted us as she marched over to our table, dressed like an early 2000 Bratz doll. Just the sight of this bitch made me want to jump up and smack the fuck out of her slutty ass, but I refused to show out in public and give this bitch any satisfaction. Instead, I just killed the bitch with silence, not even acknowledging her ass.

"Chello, what the fuck are you even doing here?" Beautiful questioned while I continued sipping on my drink.

"Damn, a bitch can't even come over to say hey to you hoes? I was just being courteous."

"You can cool it on the name calling."

"Oh, my bad, baby mama. I didn't mean no disrespect. Anyway, how is the pregnancy going? Did you tell Tennessee what was up with his 'baby'?" This bitch used air quotes when she said *baby*, which meant she was definitely trying to throw shade at Beautiful for being pregnant by Tennessee. Knowing this trifling slut, she probably was fucking his ass too.

"Chello, please get the fuck up outta here, trying to start some shit, okay? Don't nobody got time for your shenanigans today."

"Aw, you ain't got time for me today? Really? Damn, you hurt my feelings, B. I thought we were cool."

"Bitch, we'll never fucking be cool again. You got life all the way fucked up."

"Oh, you feeling real tight today, huh? That's cool. A bitch about to head back to the Chi anyway. These Atlanta niggas can't fuck with a South Side bitch like me. But I'm glad I ran into y'all to say goodbye. I hope life be good to y'all down here. Oh, before I leave; Beautiful, did you let Secret know you're not really pregnant by Tennessee, and that your baby daddy is Memmo?"

"What?" I snapped my head in Beautiful's direction. I just knew this bitch didn't say what the fuck I thought she said, and for Beautiful's sake, she'd better be fucking lying.

"Oh, cousin, you thought this hoe was really pregnant by Tennessee? No, the bitch just didn't want to tell you she's been fucking your dead sister's baby daddy. They were even smashing before Diamond died."

At this point, I really wasn't hearing shit she had to say about Beautiful and Memmo, but I refused to let this goofy bitch talk crazy about my sister. About my sister's name, I'd knock any bitch out. Grabbing Beautiful's glass of water, I didn't blink twice, throwing it right in Chello's face. I tried to drown that dumb ass hoe for coming at me sideways, talking shit about my sister. Her mouth was too fucking reckless, and I was really sick of her ass.

"Bitch, don't you ever in your fucking life mention my sister's name out of your dick suckers, bitch! You better get the fuck out of here before I dust your stupid ass."

"Oh, you big mad, huh, cousin? I was just speaking facts. I guess I should let you know that I was the one who falsified that DNA test of your son. That crazy bitch, Tabatha, paid me a good penny for my services."

"Chello, you really are a low-down, slimy, dick-sucking skeezer. You really are that envious of me that you would stoop so low to make Priest think he's not my son's father. Bitch, you're sick, and you need help."

"Envious? Bitch, why would I be envious of you? Look at you and look at me."

"Every fucking thing I have, you want it, bitch. You wanted Von, but all he did was use your stupid ass. You attempted to slide up on Priest, but he would never fuck a hoe like you with a sick dick, and now, you wanna play games with Tabatha."

"I really just did it for the money. I don't give two fucks who your baby daddy is."

"Chello, why don't you just get the fuck up out of here? All you do is stir up bullshit, with your raggedy ass."

"Don't get mad at me, bitch. I'm just letting my cousin know you ain't no better than me. You're a slimy, sneaky, snake ass, thot bitch just like me. You love to try and turn Secret against me when you've been snaking her this entire time. Get your fucking life, Beautiful. And Secret, you need to watch that bitch 'cause she's probably fucking Priest too."

"Girl, bye! Get the fuck out of here! Bye, bitch!"

"Oh, and Beautiful, you might want to watch your back 'cause Tennessee know that ain't his baby. Enjoy your life, bitches!"

As Beautiful yelled out curse words to Chello as she skated out of the restaurant in the same manner that she came in, her words were finally dawning on me. Not once did Beautiful deny Chello's allegations that she was pregnant by Memmo and not Tennessee. I was trying hard to not overreact, especially because she was sitting in front of me, pregnant, but I could feel my blood begin to boil with rage. Our friendship was already trying to be repaired from her keeping Chello and Von's affair from me, and now she was sleeping around with Memmo. How much more bullshit would I have to endure?

"Can you believe that bitch? Always showing up to start some bullshit."

"B, is it true? About you and Memmo? Are you fucking him? Is that his baby?"

"Look, Secret, before you go crazy, just hear me out. I wanted to tell you a long time ago about me and Memmo, but he wouldn't let me. I didn't want to keep it from you, but we just didn't know how you would react."

"How I would react? Bitch, are you serious? You're fucking my sister's baby daddy, and I'm supposed to be cool with that?" It was taking every bit of strength I had to not reach across this table and choke the shit out of this bitch.

"With all due respect, Secret, Diamond is gone. It's not like I was messing around with Memmo behind her back and to be honest, you're my best friend, not Diamond. I just never pursued anything with Memmo out of respect for you. Whatever Memmo and I have going on doesn't really have anything to do with you."

"Hoe, you're lucky your pregnant right now, or I'd be mopping the floor with your dog ass. How dare you sit across from me and act like what you're doing ain't fucked up. My sister treated you like you were her own sister, and this is how you repay her? Bitch, you got me fucked up." I grabbed my purse and attempted to make a quick exit out of the restaurant, and as far away from Beautiful's ass, before I smacked the fuck out of this bitch.

"Secret, how can you be mad at me? It ain't like Memmo was your boyfriend. I'm sorry, but Diamond is gone, and she ain't coming back. Why should I have to withhold my feelings just because he's your sister's baby daddy? He and Diamond weren't even together."

"It's about loyalty; something you don't know shit about. And to keep me from beating the fuck out of you all across this place, I'm going to leave. Do yourself a favor and stay the fuck away from me, you back-stabbing, snake ass bitch."

I damn near ran out of the restaurant, trying to put as much distance between me and Beautiful as I could because I could feel my hands wrapping around her neck and squeezing until I felt her soul leave her body. This was the second time this bitch betrayed me, and I'd be damned if I gave her a third time to do it again. I was so over motherfuckers continuing to play with my heart and my emotions. I just wanted to scream. After all the shit we'd been through since we met to mend our friendship, this bitch had the audacity to be fucking Memmo right under my nose like that shit was cool. Even though Beautiful and Diamond weren't blood related, my sister treated Beautiful the same way she did me. She looked out for us, put us up on game, and always had our backs. My sister even fought bitches over Beautiful, and for her to act like she and Diamond never had a close relationship was straight up bullshit.

I would have respected that bitch ten times more if she would have just been a woman about it and told me up front that she wanted to start dating Memmo, but it was the fact that the bitch tried to hide it from me. That was the problem. And to go as far as to tell me she was carrying another man's baby was wild as fuck. To say I was pissed off was an understatement because I put my trust in someone who had already betrayed me once. I was foolish enough to think the bitch changed, but clearly, don't shit change but the seasons. This time, I was washing my hands of Beautiful for good this time. Her bitch ass ain't have shit else to say to me ever again in this lifetime.

From Bad to Worse

Tennessee

I paced back and forth in my living room with my gun in my hand, waiting on this lying ass hoe to show up. Chello must have told Beautiful that I was aware she was trying to play me like I was some goofy ass nigga or something because she had been blowing up my phone and texting me for the last few days, trying to explain her side of things. I honestly didn't want to see or hear a damn thing she had to say 'cause one thing I didn't like was a flaw ass, snake ass hoe. What I really wanted to do was roll up on the bitch and beat the fuck out of her goofy ass, but I was holding my composure for as long as I could.

A few minutes passed by, and I heard a car door shut outside of my front door. I looked out of the window to see Beautiful stepping out of her car. I quickly cocked my gun to make sure I had one in the chamber before I let this bitch up in my crib. Since she was fucking with the opps and supposedly carrying his baby, it ain't no telling what this hoe was up to. The bitch was probably trying to set me up or some shit. But one thing I knew for certain was if she was coming here with the truth, I just might have to lay this hoe down. Shit, I needed my lick back after Memmo and that goofy ass nigga Von put two slugs in my bitch back in Chicago. All these motherfuckers were about to learn to stop playing on motherfucking top.

Soft taps came at the door before I unlocked it and peeped out of the small opening to make sure she was by herself before I let her ass in. Just the sight of her made me want to knock her fuckin' teeth down her throat, but I was going to try my damnedest to let her explain before I went silly on this bitch.

"So, what's up? How you doing?" I started off the conversation, but I could tell by the way she looked at me, shit was about to get real.

"Why don't we cut to the chase, and let's go ahead and address the elephant in the room. I know Chello's diarrhea mouth ass told you about me and Memmo. So, there's no need for you to act like you give a fuck about me, trying to be all nice and shit."

"Hold the fuck up. You need to watch your fucking tone with me. You the one running 'round here telling me I got a fucking baby on the way when you failed to mention you fucking with an opp ass nigga. Don't come up in my shit with an attitude, bitch."

"See? And that's exactly why I'm fucking with a real man 'cause you're too fucking disrespectful. I only came over here to let you know what was up and to cut ties, so neither one of us have to clean up pretenses."

"Is that right? So, tell me what's up then."

"The truth is, I only started fucking with you as a means to keep tabs on you for Memmo. He's the one who wants to smoke your bitch ass. And believe me, I fucking hated every second I had to be near your broke ass. But now that you know what's up, I guess we can both move the fuck on."

"You know what, bitch? You talking real greasy out the mouth like a motherfucker won't knock your head between the washer and dryer. I would advise you to watch how the fuck you talk to me."

"Whatever, Tennessee. Look, that's all I have to say to you. Anything else you need to get off your chest? 'Cause this is probably the last fucking time you'll ever see me."

"I just got one question. Who's the baby's daddy?" I stared

at her with burning intensity in my eyes. I already knew the answer, but I needed to hear it come out of her mouth. Since she wanna pop up in my crib, talking all reckless to me. She'd just unleashed the motherfucking savage in me and didn't even know it.

"Memmo is my baby's father, if you must know. You think I would have kept this motherfucker if it was yours? Please."

That was all I needed to hear. Pulling my gun from my back pocket, I swung as hard as I could, smacking her dead in the face, watching her body drop instantly to the floor. Followed by a few swift kicks to the abdomen, I had this bitch curled up in the fetal position, screaming out in agony.

"Stoooopp! Stoooop!"

"Stop what? Bitch, don't cry now. You wasn't crying when you was just boasting and talking all that big shit to me. The fuck you gotta say now, hoe?!" I stomped her ass a few more times before I held the gun at her head.

"You're gonna kill my baby." She sobbed, but her tears ain't mean a damn thing to me. I didn't give a fuck about her hoe ass or that bastard ass baby. This was a lesson for her to never try and play a real nigga 'cause I was the wrong motherfucker to try and run game on.

"Bitch, you think I give a fuck?! Fuck you and that baby, you dirty pussy ass bitch. I should knock your fucking lights out right now, but I ain't gonna do that. I do want you to tell your boyfriend a message for me." I let off two shots in her stomach and one in the cheek. "Tell that fuck nigga stop playing with me."

Picking up her phone, I used her thumbprint to unlock it. Then, I scrolled down her text messages until I found Memmo's number to send him a message.

Come get yo hoe. She bleeding on my living room floor.

Dropping the phone down next to her, I spit in that bitch's face and left her lying unconscious on the floor.

After I handled Beautiful's bitch ass, I went to my number one lounge, popped me a few Percs and drank until my vision went blurry. For some strange reason, I had a feeling that I wasn't going to be around much longer. I had racked up more enemies than I could count after shutting niggas' lil' ass trap houses down. Then, I still had to worry about that dead motherfucker, Von, lurking around this bitch somewhere, and now, his bitch ass brother was going to be on my ass too. But one thing about me, I was never a scary motherfucker, and I damn sure wasn't about to run from any motherfucker. If they wanted war, then war is what they were going to get. And if I died, then I just hope the Lord let me in them pearly gates.

Next thing I knew, I was woken up out of my sleep with some loud ass banging on the door. Looking around, trying to see where the fuck I was, there were two bad ass bitches laying on both sides of me in a hotel room. My head felt like it was being weighed down by a ton of bricks, and whoever the fuck was banging on the door only added to the pounding of my head. Who the fuck knew I was here, and why the fuck were they trying to beat the fucking door down?

It took me a minute to crawl out of the bed and throw a towel around my naked ass so I could see who the hell this was at the door. Looking out of the peephole, I saw Priest standing on the other side of the door with a mean mugging look on his face.

"Tennessee, open up this motherfucking door before I kick this bitch down!" Priest roared with much animosity in his voice. He was clearly pissed off about something.

"Hold the fuck up, man! The fuck is you knocking like you the fucking police for?" I yelled back as I opened the door to let him in.

"Nigga, you done lost your motherfucking mind or some?" Before I could get a grip on what was going on, Priest had dropped me on my ass in half of a second.

"The fuck is wrong with you, nigga? Fuck is you jumping

on me for?" I ain't even gonna lie, even though I was hung over over like a motherfucker, I knew a monster when I saw one, and the look in Priest's eyes was like he was ready to tear my ass into shreds. Priest was always one of those niggas who was calm and in control, but the second a motherfucker tested his gangster and pushed him over the edge, that motherfucker turned into something worse than the Hulk, Freddy Krueger and all of them other scary bitches in one. When he got like this, I wasn't really trying to fuck with him.

"Nigga, what the fuck was you thinking shooting up Secret's house? You could have killed her, T! Did you fucking think about that?"

This nigga was yelling so fucking loud, I wouldn't be surprised if the other guests called the police on his crazy ass. My two bitches had been woken up out of their sleep and looked confused as fuck about what was going on. Hell, I was still trying to figure out why this nigga was so upset with me.

"Man, you tripping right now. I don't know what the fuck you even yelling for."

"I tell you what; you got two minutes to get your bitches up outta here and get your ass dressed before I beat the fuck out of you in this bitch while these hoes watch."

My bitches moved quicker than I could even say anything, rushing to get their shit and getting the fuck out of dodge. They wanted no parts of the wrath of Priest and to be honest, neither did I. It took me a minute to try and get my bearings and find my pants to put on so Priest and I could talk about whatever the fuck had him so pissed off. Make no mistake about it, I was far from pussy, and nobody walking this earth put fear in my heart, but the last thing I wanted was to have a fist fight with my cousin. I knew that nigga was something lethal with his hands and how weak my ass was feeling right now, it was guaranteed he'd whoop the shit out of my ass.

After I slipped into my boxers and jeans, I threw some cold

water on my face to wake the hell up, but I was still feeling drunk as fuck. When I walked out of the bathroom, Priest was standing by the door with his arms folded across his chest. To anyone else, he would have seemed to be his regular, calm, cool self, but I took one look at his face and could see his eyes as red as the devil and filled with rage. I didn't know whether I should sit down or square up with this nigga 'cause he seemed like he was ready to rumble instead of talk.

"You mind telling me what the fuck is going on and why you showed up here banging on the door like the fucking police?"

"You gon' need the fucking police to get here and save your ass after I beat the shit out of you. What the fuck is wrong with you, nigga? You got a death wish or some shit?"

"Look, man, you gonna have to slow up on all the threats and tell me what you so mad about. As you can see, a nigga was drunk as fuck last night, and my memory ain't worth shit right now."

"I'm talking about you going on a fucking rampage and doing a drive-by at Secret's house. I'm talking about you damn near killing an innocent person, my son's mother to be precise."

"Priest, man, I wasn't even going after Secret, bro. I just wanted that goofy ass fuck boy, B.K. I had been looking for that nigga ever since he snuck me, and when I spotted him and Von standing outside, I took the opportunity to knock both of them motherfuckers out."

"Nigga, you sound stupid as fuck. I been told your slow ass to cool the fuck down on all that extra shit, but you don't listen for shit. Nigga, Secret was standing out there with them when you started blasting. Suppose you shot her and not B.K. What if my son was home?"

"Well, what you want me to do about it? That shit is over with now. Your bitch is safe, and your son wasn't even there."

I probably should have used my words differently 'cause Priest obviously didn't appreciate me calling his beloved Secret a bitch. The nigga moved at the speed of lightning, hitting me with a two-piece before I could register what the fuck was happening.

"I warned you before to watch your fucking mouth when you talking to me, nigga. I don't know what the fuck you got going on, but you better get your shit together before somebody lay you the fuck down. Don't ever disrespect my fucking family or put the people I love in harm's way again, or I swear on everything I love, I'll kill you, motherfucker."

"Oh, so you want to kill me? Your blood? Over a piece of pussy? Man, fuck you, Priest! You bitch ass nigga, you never had my fucking back anyway. Nigga, I was the one who always had to carry you. I made sure you were good in the streets and nobody fucked with you. I always been there for you, no matter what, but you could never return the fucking favor 'cause you was too busy being a bitch boy, sucking up to Von, hoping he didn't take your bitch away from you. Nigga, I don't need you or nobody else. I'm my own fucking army, nigga. Fuck you and fuck the rest of them niggas too."

"I'm done with you, T. You so fucking wrapped up in trying to make money but being a fucking dummy, going about business the wrong way. Nigga, I refuse to ever let you drag me into some shit and risk losing my family. I love you 'cause you my cousin, but I ain't got shit else to do with you. Stay the fuck away from me and mine, or Von and the rest of them niggas will be the least of your fucking worries."

"I ain't ever been scared to die. Y'all niggas want smoke? I'm on whatever the fuck they on. Tell them fuck niggas to come see me."

Locked Up

Tabatha

The day had finally come, and I couldn't be more excited. After being away from my daughter for all this time and having to have supervised visitation, we were going before the judge so he could grant my daughter to come back home to me. My little stunt with the DNA test didn't go as I'd hoped it would, but it didn't even matter because one way or another, I was getting my family back. I was laying low, playing by the rules and not causing a scene to give the courts any excuse to keep Aaliyah away from me a day longer. As hard as it was for me to play nice and keep my cool when I saw Priest, I had no other choice but to act like I had the sense God gave me to show the judge, and Priest, I'd changed. Now, all was left was to get through this day and by the night fall, my family and I would be under one roof.

As I sat in my chair next to my lawyer, I waited anxiously for the judge to appear from his chambers to hand down his ruling. Both Priest and Aaliyah were here to support me, and I couldn't have been happier to see their faces. I tried not to pay much attention to them just so no one else could say I was behaving out of order; I couldn't afford any more heat on my end from anyone if I had any hopes of getting my husband and daughter back.

Ten minutes had passed, and the judge had finally made his way in the courtroom. After the bailiff called for us to rise, my heart began to race like I was Flo-Jo running the 100-meter dash. My palms were moist, and I could feel tiny beads of sweat popping up on my forehead as the judge rambled on, giving on overview of what'd been going on for the past month. I wanted to yell out and tell his old ass to hurry the fuck up and give his ruling, but that would only reflect negatively on my behalf, so I just bit my tongue and stayed quiet.

"After going over the documents from this case, I do believe that the paternal party has performed exceedingly above satisfactory with regards to caring for his daughter. And I must say, I do see a change in maternal party's behavior; however, I do not believe a month's time can change the state of your mentality. I do believe the defendant is a malignant narcissist who would do and act in any way to get what she wants, and when she is rejected, such as the way her husband rejected her, she becomes unstable. So, with that being said, I am going to reward Mr. Carter full custody of the child indefinitely. Mrs. Carter, I am ordering you to attend weekly mental health outpatient counseling, and in ninety days, we will resume a check-in status."

"Are you fucking kidding me?! NO! This is bullshit! I WANT MY FUCKING DAUGHTER BACK NOW!" At this point, I was irate as I stood to my feet, screaming at the judge. He was out of his senile ass mind if he thought I was just going to go with the flow on that dumb ass ruling.

"Counselor, control your client, or I will hold her in contempt."

"NO, FUCK YOU! You can't take my baby way from me!" My attorney attempted to calm me down, but I wasn't trying to hear nobody. This wasn't the way this shit was supposed to go.

"Mrs. Carter, I'm warning you."

"You're not taking my baby away from me." Rushing past my attorney, I took off running in the direction of Priest and Aaliyah, but he quickly grabbed her and exited the courtroom. Before I could make it to the door, three officers threw my ass to the ground and placed me in hand restraints. All I could remember was hearing myself screaming and crying out loud, begging the judge to give my daughter back to me, but none of that worked. My baby was gone, and my ass was put back into a cold, lonely ass cell.

The judge held me in jail for thirty fucking days before he allowed me back into his courtroom again. To be honest, I really didn't give two fucks what he had to say to me, if it didn't involve him changing his mind and giving my baby back to me. I know there were times when I behaved a little erratically, but it was all out of love. I loved my husband, I loved my daughter, and I only wanted us to be a family. Everything I did was for my family, and it killed me that no one wanted to take the time to understand my side of things. But if nobody wanted to hear me out, I would just have to make them see that I would stop at nothing to get my family back.

"Mrs. Carter, the behavior you displayed in my courtroom was precisely the type of behavior a malignant narcissist displays, and it will not be tolerated in my courtroom. Do you understand me?"

"No, I do understand, nor do I give a fuck to understand whatever you have to say."

"And that attitude is why you don't have your daughter, and as long as I have anything to do with this case, it will stay as such. Furthermore, I am ordering you to serve one hundred and twenty days of inpatient psychiatric treatment at the Emory Health Institute. The slightest deviation from my orders and you will find yourself locked away in a correctional facility for the next fifteen years. Now, please get this woman out of my courtroom."

The judge could say whatever the fuck he wanted, but I'd be damned if any human being walking this earth denied me my daughter and my husband. I'd play it cool for the time being, but I already had something cooking in my head for every single motherfucker who played a part in trying to keep my family away from me, starting with that fat, slimy bitch, Secret, and her fucking son. They would be the first two to go.

Back in Blood

Von

It took a lot for me to not hunt that bitch ass nigga, Tennessee, down after that hoe ass stunt he pulled, shooting up Secret's place. I knew he would have been expecting me to wild out and retaliate immediately on his ass, but I laid low. Taking this fuck nigga out was going to be one of the best things I ever did, and I couldn't afford to make a single mistake. Moving too prematurely would cost me a golden opportunity, so I stayed quiet and watched this nigga's every move until the time was perfect. And the second I caught this bitch ass nigga lacking, I was going to stretch his ass.

Since the nigga laid B.K.'s snake ass down, he was acting like he was the nigga in these streets. I watched his nigga run around the city like a fucking macho man, being the typical flashy ass goofy he always was. One thing this nigga had a bad ass habit of was creating a routine. One of the golden rules to being heavy in the streets was to never get too comfortable and most importantly, never ever form a routine 'cause you never know who the fuck is watching your ass. But this nigga was too fucking cocky and stupid to realize what the fuck he was doing.

It didn't even take me long to pick up on this nigga's whereabouts 'cause he did the same bullshit every day. Leaving his hotel room, dropping off work, and hitting up the lounge was his daily cycle. After watching the nigga for only two days, I knew exactly where he would be at any given time of the day. And tonight, it was time for this shit to come to an end. I was prepared for whatever because the second I laid eyes on his ass, it was a wrap.

I patiently sat in my rental car in the parking lot of the lounge Tennessee was in, getting fucked up. Some local rapper niggas were having an after party and of course, this nigga followed where hoes would be shaking ass. A cute lil' thot bitch I met about a week ago who worked at the lounge knew Tennessee very well and had a problem with his cheap ass 'cause he never liked to tip her after she wouldn't give him no ass. I threw a few dollars at her and got her to keep an eye on him and who he was rolling with tonight, just in case I needed some back up. Per usual, he rolled up with a bunch of hoes and had been getting drunk and high off his ass all fucking night. The nigga even tried to show up the rappers that came through by buying the bar out like he was some type of God or some shit.

It was nearly three in the morning, and the only thing I could think of was laying this fuck nigga down. I made sure my Glock 45 was loaded with hollow points with one resting in the chamber and secured my bulletproof vest, just in case the nigga tried to shoot me back. I had a ski mask on but debated on whether or not I would use it 'cause I wanted my face to be the last thing that fuck nigga saw before he took his last breath.

A few minutes later, my phone dinged, signaling I had a message coming in. It was the bitch I had watching Tennessee texting me that he was on his way out the door with a groupie bitch. It was go time. Pulling my mask over my face and throwing my hoodie over my head, I watched the front door intently, waiting for the nigga to come out. Right on cue, the door swung open, and I spotted Tennessee stumbling out with two bitches on both sides of him. My blood started boiling instantly, and my heart began to beat like snare drums against my chest. I ain't ever wanted to kill a motherfucker as bad as I wanted to kill Tennessee's ass. This fuck nigga had taken too much from me, and now it was his time to return the favor.

The nigga never saw me coming as I snuck up from behind him and hit his ass in both of his legs, watching him drop to the ground, screaming in agony. Both of them hoes took off running back inside the club, leaving his ass to fend for himself. Stepping up to him, I kicked his ass as hard as I could in his rib cage, forcing him to turn over on his back.

"Turn your bitch ass over, goofy. The fuck you gotta say now?" I held the gun directly between his eyeballs and revealed my face to him.

"Bitch, I was wondering if you had the balls to come for me. You think I'm scared to die? Do what the fuck you gotta do, bitch."

"Oh, trust me, I am. I just wanted you to see my face and know I'm the last motherfucker you ever gonna see. Rest in piss, motherfucker." I let off three rounds in his chest and hit him twice in the head. I started to spit on his bitch ass, but I wasn't trying to leave no DNA on him.

Racing back to my car, I did the dash out of the parking lot, trying to get the fuck out of dodge. I heard the police sirens in the distance getting closer, and I quickly whipped that bitch in the parking lot behind a Mexican restaurant. I switched out of my hoodie, ski mask and jeans, threw them motherfuckers in the dumpster, and doused them with lighter fluid before setting fire to them. Once I heard the sirens pass by, I made my way towards my brother's house. Now that Tennessee's fuck ass was gone, it was time for me to get the fuck up outta Atlanta. I came, I saw, and I motherfucking conquered.

Priest

I rolled over to check the time, and it was going on six o'clock in the morning. For some weird ass reason, I hadn't been able to sleep an ounce; I just tossed and turned all fucking night. Something was troubling my spirit, and I couldn't understand why. The bullshit that transpired between me and Tennessee was weighing heavy on me, and as badly as I wanted to call and apologize to make this shit right with him, I just couldn't. Tennessee was more than just a cousin to me; the nigga was like my brother, and I hated to be at odds with him. But the way he was behaving lately wasn't cool. The nigga was acting out of order, and I couldn't stand for that shit. For once, I just wanted him to listen to me and take heed before he got himself involved in some shit that nobody could help him out of — especially now that Von was on the loose again.

Creeping out of bed, I went to the bathroom to empty my bladder and peeped in Aaliyah's room to make sure she was still sound asleep. The only thing I was missing was my boy, Cross, and my baby, Secret. I felt incomplete when Secret left for a few weeks, and it was just my babies and me. There was no greater feeling in the world than having my kids under one roof, and if Secret would stop being so fucking stubborn, we could make this shit official once and for all. But it was all good; sooner than later, she was going to be right back where she belonged — with a real nigga.

Since I was the only one up, I figured I could use this time to work out and try to ease my mind from whatever was eating at me. But before I could even get started, I hard knock came at my door. I don't know why, but my stomach instantly tightened, and I felt a wave of sorrow rush through me. Damn, I hope nothing happened to Secret or Cross, and I damn sure hoped nothing was going on with Tennessee's ass. The knock came again; this time a little harder, causing my feet to move quicker to open the door. Looking through the peephole, my stomach dropped down to my feet when I saw two police officers standing at my door. I didn't even want to hear whatever they had to say or whatever they were here for. I really just wanted to turn around and go back to bed, but I couldn't.

"Yeah?" I asked, creeping my head through the small opening.

"I'm sorry to disturb you so early, but we're looking for a Priest Carter? Is that you?"

"Yeah, that's me? What's up?"

I could tell immediately that something was definitely wrong by how the officer shifted his eyes from me to his partner.

"Um, do you know a gentleman by the name of Tennessee Anderson?"

"That's my cousin. What the fuck he done got into now?"

"Mr. Carter, unfortunately, Mr. Anderson was fatally shot around three o'clock this morning. His body was discovered outside of the Monaco Lounge. He'd suffered several shots, two in the leg, three in the torso, and two in the head. We believe he passed almost instantly."

I honestly didn't hear anything else the police were saying after I heard the words 'fatally shot'. I could see their mouths moving, but it was like I went deaf. My whole body went numb from my head to my feet, and I didn't know what to think or how to feel. I felt like I was in a bad dream, and I couldn't figure out how to wake up. It was taking my mind forever to process what my ears just heard.

"Mr. Carter? Mr. Carter?" I must have been staring off for a while because the officer started shaking my arm to snap me out of my trance. "Sir, do you know of anyone who would have wanted to harm Mr. Anderson? Did he have any known enemies that you can think of?"

"My cousin was heavy in the streets, and he was making a lot of bad decisions that I knew would come back to haunt him. But I wasn't a part of that lifestyle, so I can't tell you who he hung around or who he rubbed the wrong way."

"We do know that Mr. Anderson was wanted for questioning about another shooting where a young, pregnant woman by the name of Beautiful Morales was shot in the face. Do you know anything about that?"

"No, I don't. I know they were fucking around and whatnot, but like I said, he was my cousin, but we weren't seeing eye to eye for the past few months. He was into some shit I wanted no parts of. So, whatever he was doing in his personal life, I can't really tell you much about it."

"I understand. And again, we're very sorry for your loss, and if there is anything else you can think of, please don't hesitate to give us a call. In the meantime, there're a few detectives still processing the scene, and once they're done, Mr. Anderson's belongings will be at the station for you to come and retrieve."

"Where is his body? Can I see him?"

"He's down at the county morgue. Once an autopsy is completed, he will be released to family. I'll make sure to give you a call once you're able to go down and see him to perform a procedural identification."

"Thanks. I appreciate it."

"Once again, our condolences to you, and if there is any new information we come across, we'll be sure to let you know."

I was still in shock when the officers left. I didn't know what to think, feel, or how to even begin to process this shit. Ever since Tennessee came to Atlanta, I had been worried about him. Atlanta was like a watered down Chicago, but motherfuckers 'round here didn't play about their money or their business, and being an outsider was a double whammy. I always feared something like this would happen to him, but I tried my best to talk him out of this whole street life, kingpin shit. The nigga just wouldn't listen to me.

I knew Tennessee made a hell of a lot of enemies since being here, but there was only one person who could've been responsible for this shit, and that was Von. He'd warned me that he was coming for Tennessee, and I guess he finally caught him lacking. God knows Tennessee meant a lot to me, and I never wanted to see his life get snatched away from him, but I felt like there was nothing else I could do. I put him up on game and told him Von was coming for his ass, but none of that shit fazed him. How the fuck could I save a motherfucker who thought they were invincible?

As I sat and tried to give my brain time to work through this shit, I felt so hopeless. What was I supposed to do now? Aside from my kids and my mama, Tennessee was all I had left. We fussed a lot, and I disagreed with most of his bullshit, but nobody else would ever have my back the way he did. Now, I was starting to feel the pain and the guilt of losing yet another person so close to me. I could have done more to save him, but instead, I felt like I led my cousin out to the slaughter.

Sitting here, all by myself, with a million emotions running through me and negative thoughts clouding my head, I felt like if I didn't talk to somebody, I was going to explode, and I couldn't afford to break down with my baby in the next room sleeping. She was already going through a lot, not having her mother around right now; she didn't need to see her daddy losing it too. I didn't know what else to do, so I just dropped to my knees and starting praying, asking God for strength and understanding. Why did I have to keep going through so much shit, losing the ones who meant the most to me? Why was I designated to be the strongest one everyone else could lean on, but when I was reaching my breaking point, there was nobody around I could call? How much more was a nigga supposed to take?

I wanted to cry, scream, and hit something as hard as I could just to release some of the pain I was feeling but even still, it probably wouldn't help. I was getting to a point where I was starting to get so tired and worn down. I didn't know how to begin to pick up the broken pieces of my heart but somehow, I knew I couldn't just lay down right now. And as I tried to focus and find some inner strength to deal with this shit, I could feel the presence of my granny surrounding me, her spirit covering me like a blanket.

"I need you more than ever, granny. I'm getting tired, man. I'm tired of losing people. I need help, granny. Tell me what I'm supposed to do."

Another knock came at the door as I waited for an answer from my granny. She was the only one who'd have the perfect words to say at a time like this. Her hugs alone would have helped ease the pain. But since she couldn't be here with me in the physical, I guess she sent someone else in her place 'cause when I opened the door, Secret was standing on the other side. I tried so hard not to burst into tears when I saw her face, but I could feel them trying to force their way out. She never said a word; instead, she just wrapped her arms around me and held me as tightly as she could. The smell of her skin, the warmth of her body, and the coolness of her breath washing over my neck was something I'd been longing for, for so long. At that moment, I could feel the love pouring from her body and into mine, leaving me no other choice but to just break down.

"I'm here for you, baby. I promise, I got you," Secret whispered as she held on to me like her life depended on it, never letting me go.

The Final Goodbye

Secret

It was so hard to watch Priest go through the pain of losing Tennessee. Some days, he would wake up in a good mood, laughing and joking about the good times they shared together and other days, he could barely hold himself together. As long as I'd known Priest, I had never seen him so defeated and beaten down; it was like he was drowning in pain. Although Tennessee wasn't my favorite human being in the world, no one deserved to be murdered in cold blood, and Priest damn sure didn't deserve to have to bury another family member. Regardless of the bullshit we'd gone through in the past, I felt obligated to be by his side through all of this because I knew what it felt like to lose someone you loved. I'd felt that type of pain before, and it was a pain that never went away; you just learn to live with it as the days go by. Any time I needed Priest to be there for me, he never hesitated, so it was only right that I return the favor.

After two weeks of the police doing their investigation, they had finally released Tennessee's body over to Priest so that he could have him flown to Chicago to be buried. Seeing Priest break down when he saw his cousin's body in the morgue and listening to him cry out in anguish broke my heart into a million pieces. Priest had always been so strong and possessed the ability to put his feelings and emotions aside to carry everyone else's burdens. But losing Tennessee crippled him and for the first time, I had to watch this mighty man, fall into shambles without the first clue of how to put himself back together.

Cross and I had practically moved in with Priest and Aaliyah because I couldn't bear the thought of leaving him all alone. I couldn't lie, though, being around Priest every single day brought me back to why I fell so hard and so fast for him. Even through all of the tribulations he was facing, he still found the time to just acknowledge me. Sometimes, I even caught him staring at me the way he used to back when we first started going together. He would look at me like I was the most beautiful person in the world. It amazed me how at his most vulnerable state, he still found a way to make me feel special without forcing himself on me.

Once I helped Priest get all of Tennessee's affairs in order, it was time to fly to Chicago to give him a proper burial. I was anxious to get back to the Chi to see Abuela, and I knew she was going to be ecstatic to see Cross again. Having both Abuela and Crystal around would also give me and Priest time alone to sort through all the things we both left unsaid. I had already closed the book on Von and my relationship, Tennessee took care of B.K., and the only thing left to do was make things right with Priest. God in heaven knew from the first time I'd given Priest my heart, I never really got it back. I was just too afraid to acknowledge a love as real and as raw as Priest's.

Due to Tennessee's collection of enemies in Chicago, Priest didn't even bother having a church service or anything. He and I just had a private moment at the burial site. It was always hard watching your loved ones be lowered into the ground with dirt thrown over them, but I was just happy I could be here for Priest.

"Shit still don't seem right, man. My nigga really gone," Priest said, watching the casket drop into its final resting place.

"It's crazy, but Tennessee was always so wild and lived his life regardless of the consequences."

"I just feel like I could have done more. I should have been there to protect him. I knew this shit was coming, and I tried to warn him about it, but he was just so fucking hardheaded. The nigga acted like he wanted to die or something."

"You can't keep blaming yourself, Priest. Tennessee was a grown man who made his own decisions, right or wrong. He what he wanted, when and how he wanted to without any regard for anybody else, including you. It's not your fault he created this outcome for himself."

"Isn't though? Secret, I knew Von wasn't going to stop until he laid T down. Am I not just as responsible for his death? I could have stopped this shit, man. Just like me and Von came to peaceful agreement to put all this shit in the past, they could have done the same thing. It didn't have to come to this."

"The difference is, you had the mindset to leave the past in the past and move on; neither Von nor Tennessee were willing to let go of the beef until one of them ended up dead. Still, that doesn't fall on you."

"I'm just sick of this shit, man. I can't handle no more bullshit."

"Priest, listen to me, you are an amazing man. You are the best father that Aaliyah and Cross could ever ask for. You gotta stop letting other people's problems dictate your life. You only owe loyalty to your kids and yourself. Quit trying to be superman. You are enough just the way you are."

"Just not enough for you, though."

And there it is. The statement that was about to open up the can of worms I'd been trying to figure out how to spill. I'd been wanting to have a real heart-to-heart with Priest for the longest, but the time just never seemed to be on my side. Whenever I'd build up my nerve to speak to him, something would always block my way. And being in the cemetery damn sure wasn't my ideal place to hash everything out, but this was the only place we both seemed to get anything out these days.

"That's not true. In fact, you've always been more than enough for me. There's never been a time when I needed you and you weren't there for me. Our falling out had nothing to do with you and everything to do with me."

"It ain't a second that goes by that I don't think about some of the decisions I made when it comes to us. When I first met you, your spirit spoke to me, and my whole body lit up like the Fourth of July any time I was around you. You made me feel a way I'd never felt before in my life, and all I wanted was just to be with you. I was willing to do whatever it took to have you, but I never took into consideration that you were fresh out of a relationship. We just hit the ground running, and the first time we hit a brick wall, neither one of knew how to handle it. I was so focused on not losing you, I didn't give your heart a chance to heal from that past situation."

"Priest, you scared me. Your love, dedication, loyalty; just the whole person you are scared the shit out of me. I've never had the kind of love you showed me. You always had a way of making me feel like nothing and no one else in this universe mattered to me. When I needed a listening ear, you were present. When I cried, you wiped my tears. You were my protector, and you gave me strength and unconditional love even when I didn't deserve it. And when I thought I could lose that type of love forever, I retreated and ran back to what was normal to me. I pushed you away because I was afraid that I couldn't love you the way loved me, and I never ever wanted to hurt you again." Tears rolled down my face as I let my truth be known. It felt like a ton had been lifted off my shoulders after I finally released everything that I'd held inside my heart for Priest.

Walking up close to me, Priest gently wiped away my river of tears with the back of his hand. "I never needed you to be perfect for me, Secret. I just needed you. Your love has always been enough for me."

"I never meant to hurt you, Priest. And if I'm being honest, I never stopped loving you. I never stopped wanting you."

"And I don't ever want you to stop." Pulling me closer to

him, Priest cupped my chin and gave me the sweetest kiss I hadn't felt since the last time we were intimate with each other. Every time his lips pressed against mine, I could feel the love and passion he had for me. I could feel how much he wanted me, and, in that moment, I finally stopped running from the love I always wanted. I gave in to the man of my dreams.

One Word...Three Letters

Priest

3 Months Later...

"So, what's the update on Tabatha?"

"Well, she's been strangely quiet as of late. The judge ordered her to serve a little over three months of inpatient psychiatric treatment. I've been receiving weekly updates on her behavior, and so far, there hasn't been any major progress. She's just doing the bare minimum to be released, which is in about two more weeks."

"And what about her visits with Aaliyah?"

"She won't be able to see her until the judge grants her visitation rights. And after that rant she pulled in the courtroom, she's not the judge's favorite person right now. She'd have to show an incredible amount of behavior change to persuade the judge to show some favor."

"As long as she stays the hell away from me and my family, that's all I care about. Once she finds out that I've completely moved on from her ass, she ain't gonna take that shit lightly. So, I would appreciate it if you would do whatever you can to make sure my kids and Secret are safe."

"Will do, Mr. Carter. I'll be in touch."

"Thanks."

After I hung up with my lawyer, I stepped lightly in the

direction of the kids' room and peeped in to make sure they were still sleeping. Usually, around this time of morning, they would be up, begging for breakfast but last night, we let them stay up late, and it was going on ten in the morning, and they were both still knocked out sleep. Heading back to my room, I couldn't help but smile when I saw my beautiful Secret sleeping so peacefully. My heart was so full of love and joy, having my family back together under the same roof. The past few months had been total hell for me, but having my woman back in my life made shit ten times better.

Losing Tennessee was something I was still trying to process, but I was taking it day by day. I was still struggling with the guilt of letting Von take out my cousin and not doing much to stop it. In a sense, I felt responsible for my own cousin's death. I knew the beef between the both of them ran deep, but it was no deeper than the beef I had with Von; shit, the nigga pulled the trigger on my little brother and made a few attempts on my life because I took Secret from him. If I was able to turn the other cheek, I didn't see why they couldn't squash that petty shit they had going on. But then again, I guess it was the growth for me and not wanting to take another man's life. If I really wanted to kill Von, he damn sure wouldn't have been walking around alive and well right now. But sometimes, you just have to let certain shit go. The shit still fucked with me that my cousin didn't even try to listen to me.

The one good thing that came from all of this shit was Secret being there to help me through some of my darkest hours. I guess I had my granny to thank because I remember praying, asking her for help, and she sent Secret back to me. And when we were in Chicago, we finally had the opportunity to stop sweeping shit under the rug and say everything that needed to be said. Needless to say, I got my baby back, and there was no way in hell I was going to let her go again.

Leaning over her, I slid my hand under the sheet to caress her warm, silky smooth body while planting kisses along her bare elbow, going up to her cheek. She stirred under my embrace as a soft smile spread across her face.

"Good morning, Lil' One. You trying to sleep in or something?"

"Thanks to you. You wore me out last night."

"Don't blame me; you acted like you knew how to hang with a real nigga. Clearly, you forgot I'm big dog around this motherfucker."

"Yeah, whatever. Are the babies still sleep?"

"Um hmm. Why? You trying to go for round five?"

"You the one coming in here, disturbing my beauty sleep, so you must be trying to get something started."

"As much as I would love to, we both got shit to handle. Now, get your ass up and don't make me tell you again." I playfully slapped her on her bare ass, making it jiggle before I made my way to the bathroom to get dressed.

Today, I had something extra special for the lady of my life, and I couldn't wait to see her reaction. Since we'd been back in Atlanta, I'd been busting my ass, trying to find us the perfect home to grow our family in 'cause this lil' two bedroom we were shacked up in just wasn't hitting it. My kids deserved nothing but the best. That included having their own room, and I wanted do whatever I could to make sure my Secret didn't want for anything. So, my realtor, Angel, had finally come through with a gorgeous home on the lake in Alpharetta, and I just knew Secret was going to love it.

By the time we pulled up to the driveway of our new home, I could see Secret and the kids' faces light up like a Christmas tree. But the best was yet to come 'cause I had an even bigger surprise in store, once they saw what was waiting on the inside.

"Oh my gosh. Baby, whose house is this?" Secret asked, gazing at the big seven-bedroom home in front of us.

"Ours, if you like it."

"Ours? Baby, how in the hell can we live in something like this? I mean, I make a pretty decent penny, but you stopped the music thing so —"

"So, you asking too many questions, Lil' One. You forget I'm the motherfucking goat? I got this."

"Yeah, whatever." She rolled her eyes at me as we headed towards the front door.

As soon as she opened the door, she let out a loud screech when she saw Abuela waiting for her arrival. Although she put her best face on every single day, I knew it was hard for her to be away from her grandmother. Plus, I felt it was only right for her to be here to help us celebrate and give me her blessings.

"Abuela? Oh, my Goood! What are you doing here?" She raced to her grandmother, wrapping her arms around her tightly.

"Ahh, mi hermosa bebe. I missed you, my sweet girl."

"How did you get here?"

"Your handsome muchacho sent for me, señorita."

"Is that right?" She shot a suspicious look my way. "What exactly are y'all up to?"

"Secret, baby, you know how much I love you, right?" I walked up to her, placing both of her hands in mine.

"Yes, I know. I love you, too."

"From the very first time I saw you when we bumped into each other at the gym; I couldn't get the image of your gorgeous face out of my mind. We experienced a few bumps in the road, but my love for you never ran cold. I just wanted to tell you how much I love you and how thankful I am that I have you back in my life. Through some of my darkest hours, you have been my ray of sunshine. I never experienced a love like the one you give to me, and my heart could never beat for another being on this planet but for you. When I look into your eyes, I see my future with you, and every time you're in my presence, you still give me butterflies. I never want to spend any other day of my life without you. So…" Kneeling down to one knee, I pulled out a black box and opened it to reveal a platinum pear-shaped halo diamond engagement ring. Seeing the tears roll down Secret's face as she looked down at me with so much passion and love in her eyes, I knew for sure I had made the right decision this time.

"Will you do me the honor of becoming my wife?"

"YES! YES! YES!"

Slipping the ring on her finger, I grabbed her in my arms and kissed her as if I would never be able to kiss her lips again. The room erupted in screams and claps as our babies and Abuela cheered us on. Finally, we made it official. I wasn't going nowhere, and she damn sure wasn't going nowhere. I had the woman of my dreams in my arms, and she was ready to be my wife. The woman who deserved it was going to carry my last name, and there was not damn thing no one could do or say to take away the joy and love I had in my heart right now.

$$\mathcal{In}\ \mathcal{Awe}...\mathcal{Until}$$

Secret

"I can't believe I missed the proposal. This new job be tripping sometimes, but I'm so happy for you and my baby."

"I know. I'm still in shock myself. I just feel like I'm living in a fairytale."

"I can see. Your face is glowing, baby girl, and I know my son is as happy as a kid on Christmas. You changed his life for the better, you know."

"And he's definitely changed my life. Words can't express how happy I am to have him back."

"So, what's the plan for the wedding? Any colors in mind? Bridesmaids? Venues? What's happening?"

"Whoa, whoa, whoa. Hold up, mama Crystal; I haven't so much as thought of a date, let alone anything else. To be honest, I'm not even sure I want to have a wedding. I don't really have family, aside from my Abuela and friends."

"Oh no, baby girl. You deserve to walk down that aisle in your beautiful dress while my son waits to see his beautiful bride. It don't matter if there is no one else in the room but the two of you and your babies; y'all deserve that fairytale ending."

"I don't know. I'll have to think about it. We just moved into this new house, and weddings are crazy expensive."

"Stop trying to short change yourself, baby. We are going to have this wedding, if I have to drag you down the aisle myself.

Now, if you will excuse me, I'm going to go pick up my grandkids from school and take them for some ice cream like I promised. You, Miss Thang, get busy on your wedding list." As Mama Crystal was gathering her things to leave, a knock came at the door. When she answered it, there was delivery man standing on the other side holding a dozen of roses with a card stuck in the middle.

"Delivery for Secret Youngblood." The older gentleman stated as he attempted to hand off the roses to Mama Crystal.

"Oh no, baby, not me. That would be her." Mama Crystal pointed at me before sliding past the delivery man, making her way out to her car.

"Yeah, I'm Secret." I said, taking the roses." Taking a whiff of the aroma from the roses, I couldn't help but to smile. Priest always knew exactly how to make me feel so special. But as I opened the card, I found out rather quickly that it wasn't Priest with a kind gesture this time; it was Von.

I hope these roses ain't too much, Ma. You know a nigga ain't never been too good with all this sentimental shit. I just wanted you to know that I got a deal waiting on me in Cali. I figured it's about time I become and man and make something out this second chance at life. But no matter what, I'll always be around. And in my own special way, a nigga will always love you, ma. Make sure that nigga Priest treat you right.

Von

Reading the note from Von made my heart smile. I was genuinely happy that he found some sort od purpose in life and was willing to take full advantage of being granted a second chance to do better. The old Secret would have probably been sadden that Von was leaving again but now that we both spoke our peace and cut the ties between us in a respectable way, I felt good letting him go. As much as I will always love and care for him, I know in my heart we were just never meant to be. Finally, I was able to accept it. And now, I could focus solely on Priest and

I.

After the placed the roses in a vase on the kitchen table, I raced from the kitchen to the guest bathroom. I had been holding my piss for the longest time, but I had to wait to get a little privacy so I could take this pregnancy test. From the time we were in Chicago till now, Priest and I had been going at it like rabbits. I don't know if we both were just making up for lost time, or the chemistry between us was just undeniable, but we could barely keep our hands off of each other. Anywhere we could get a little quickie, we were getting it in. Now, my ass was sitting here looking crazy once again because my period was three weeks late.

Two and a half minutes later, I was staring at two dark pink lines in the display screen. Any other time, I probably would have been freaking out but this time around, I cried tears of joy, and I knew once Priest found out, he was going to be delirious. Having a big family was something I always wanted, and having it with Priest made things even more special. I couldn't wait till he came home to share the good news with him.

I wanted to plan something really nice and special for him, maybe cook his favorite meal, before I broke the news to him. So, I sent Crystal a text, asking if she would mind handling the kids tonight so Priest and I could have some alone time before I gathered my things to head to the grocery store. Just as I opened my front door, I was met by Beautiful, standing in front of me. The first thing I noticed was a big ass scar on the left side of her face, and she didn't look like someone who was expecting a baby.

"You must have thought I was playing when I told you I'd dust your ass if you ever came around me again."

"Listen, Secret. I am only here to say my goodbyes."

"How do you even know where the fuck I live?"

"Priest told me. Look, I don't blame you for still being upset with me. You have every right to never want to speak to me again. But after everything I've been through these past few months — getting shot by Tennessee, losing my baby, and Memmo up and I deciding to go our separate ways I feel like the best thing for me to do is just get out of town and find my own way in the world again. I've lost myself, and I know I won't be able to get back to me here in Atlanta. I only came here to say that from the bottom of my heart, I am so sorry for everything I ever did to you. As much as you may hate me right now, I never meant to hurt you, Secret. I love you and I wish you nothing but the best because you deserve it."

I hesitated for a moment before I even responded. Truthfully, in my heart, I didn't hate Beautiful, but I damn sure didn't want her ass as a fucking friend anymore. The bitch was too much of a snake for me, and I was completely over all the lies, secrets, and betrayal. I guess it was safe to say that our friendship had run its course, and it was time to say goodbye for real this time.

"Good luck with whatever this life takes you, Beautiful."

"Same to you. Congratulations on the engagement." She glanced down at my hand before turning around to walk out of my life forever.

Final Act

Tabatha

Just as the clock struck three o'clock in the morning, it was time to execute my plan. After finding out from Priest's punk ass attorney that he'd taken his name off our home and had the fucking audacity to propose to that fat ass, slimy, skank ass bitch, Secret, I was literally about to lose my shit. I'd be damned if I sat back and watched the love of my life, the only man I was destined to be with, get married to that bitch. I would rather die first and take them motherfuckers down with me. If I wasn't going to be happy with Priest, there wasn't a soul on this earth that would be happy with him.

When I heard the news and the way that goofy ass attorney smirked at me like he was happy to tell me Priest went back to that bum ass bitch, it took every ounce of restraint to not pull that motherfucker's esophagus out through his fucking nose. But that would only prolong the inevitable. I played the shit cool and pretended like I didn't give two fucks, but deep down inside, I was boiling like a lake of fire. I couldn't risk showing any sign of anger, or I would spend the next fifteen years locked away in a prison. Truth be told, I really didn't give a fuck what happened to me after I unleashed my wrath on Secret, Priest, and their punk ass son, Cross. Every single one of them motherfuckers were going to pay for the pain and misery they caused me. But until I got my hands on them, I played it cool.

Easing out of my room, I carefully made my way down to the security office where Zion's lazy ass was sure to be knocked the fuck out. When I rounded the corner, he was slumped over in the chair, snoring his ass off. The dumb ass even had his jacket thrown over the counter with his I.D. and keys hanging out. Slithering like a snake on the ground, I quietly removed his keys and his credentials so that I would be able to have access to the doors. Once I was successful, I crept back to my room to wait on Sophia's slow ass to make her rounds. She was one of the oldest, nastiest bitches to work in this facility, and I was so glad; she was about to be my first victim. But first, I made a pit stop at the medication counter and made a sweet concoction of some of the strongest drugs they had and stuck the needle in my pants.

Like clockwork, Sophia, the wicked witch, made her rounds to each room. I could hear her loud ass keys and heavy feet dragging a mile away. When she was at the next room over, I got up and sat Indian style with my back towards the door. I knew the second she saw me up, she was going to try and put me in a chokehold to lay back down, but tonight, I had something waiting on that ass. I heard my door crack open, and my adrenaline began to pump. I was ready to put this bitch's lights out for good.

"Are you really testing me tonight, Tabatha? I'm really not in the mood for your demented games tonight. Lay your ass down and go to bed. Now."

I ignored her request, which only made her all the more pissed off.

"Alright. You want to do things the hard way? Be my guest."

I counted her steps as she walked with a purpose towards me. As soon as I could feel the temperature of her body rush against me, I turned around, grabbing her by the arm as hard and tight as I could and jabbed the needle into her neck, draining the fluids. Not even ten seconds passed before she was on the floor, foaming at the mouth. Standing over her, I watched her take her very last breath with the biggest grin on my face.

"You shouldn't have been such a mean ass bitch." Hawking

up a mouth full of mucus, I spit it directly in her face.

I took her keys from her hip and went to find her locker, where I knew she kept some extra clothes. I changed into some of her old ass scrubs, pinned my hair up, and threw a nursing net over my head with a surgical mask, so no one would recognize me. Just as easy as the summer morning breeze, I walked right out of the front door without anyone even giving me a second look. The only thing on my mind was finding Secret and Priest. And as sure as the sun rose every morning, today was going to be their last day breathing.

Gone with the Wind

Secret

Just as I expected, Priest was over the moon when I told him about the pregnancy. I still couldn't believe how everything was falling into place for us, but I wouldn't trade it for love or money. Everything I had ever wanted or dreamed of had finally come to pass. Now, all I had to do was live out the rest of my life as Mrs. Priest Carter.

Mama Crystal had finally convinced me to go with having a whole ceremonious wedding, even though I was with child. I didn't exactly plan on walking down the aisle with a big ass belly in front of me, but as long as I was marrying Priest, it didn't even really matter. Neither one of us wanted to wait until after I had the baby to say 'I do', so we were planning to get married in exactly two months on April 7, which was Priest's granny's birthday. It was going to be very small and intimate at the Swan House with just our babies, Mama Crystal, and Abuela. I couldn't wait.

Today was an even more special day for me because I had an appointment at the famous Bridals by Lori. This was something I always dreamed I would be doing with my sister and my best friends, Beautiful and Chello, but I guess life had other plans for me. Going through all the bullshit I'd been through at such a young age, like losing the ones closest to me and being betrayed by the ones I thought would always have my back, opened my eyes to a lot of things and more importantly, made me grow up.

While the kids were off at school and Priest was handling

his own business, Mama Crystal and I spent the day searching for the perfect wedding dress. Since it wasn't going to be an extravagant wedding, I didn't want anything too over-the-top but still something to make a statement. I was so grateful to have Crystal step in and be there to help me through special moments like this. Since her and Priest's relationship was still being mended, it felt good to have her support us and for her and Priest to finally act as mother and son again. They both came a long way, and I was happy to see the hate and resentment gone.

Mama Crystal was enjoying a glass of champagne while she waited for me to show her the fourth dress selection of the day. Crystal completely dismissed the first three dresses, but hopefully, the fourth one was the charm. It was an eggshell, off the shoulder dress with a train and lace detail. It fitted my body perfectly, and the second I stepped in front of the mirror, I fell in love. This was definitely my dress, whether Crystal agreed or not.

"So? What do you think?" I stepped from behind the curtain to give her a view of the dress.

"Wow, Secret. Now, that is a dress, honey. You look absolutely stunning."

"You like it?"

"I love it and more importantly, I think Priest is going to love it too. This is a tear-jerking dress right here, baby."

"So, ladies, have we found the dress?" my dress consultant, Mira, asked. But before I could respond, my cell phone rang. It was Cross's daycare calling. I figured because he was just starting at this new daycare after being used to a nanny and hanging out with his sister all day, he was giving them a hard time, but as soon as I answered, I could hear panic in his teacher's voice.

"Ms. Youngblood? We need you to get down to the school as soon as possible. Please!"

"What's happening? Is my baby okay?" I was trying to stay

calm, but my nerves were beginning to take over me.

"No, ma'am, I'm afraid he's not. Your son has been kidnapped."

"WHAT?! What the hell are you talking about?"

"All we know for right now is that he was out during recess time on the playground when a lady approached him. The assistant teacher asked who she was and if she had been verified through the front office. That's when she stabbed the young woman, snatched Cross, and took off. The police were notified immediately, and when the cameras were reviewed, they noticed a band on her arm, like she'd just been discharged from a hospital or something."

"Oh my God. Oh my God." The phone slipped from my hand, and I dropped to my knees. I felt like someone had just high kicked me in my gut, knocking all the wind out of me. My head was spinning, and my airway felt like it was constricted, as if I was about to pass out at any given second.

"Secret? Secret, talk to me. What's going on?"

"C-c-call Priest. Tabatha just took my son."

We All Fall Down 2.0

Priest

I did the dash down the highway, trying to get to my son's daycare center. I didn't give two fucks about nothing and no one; all I knew was when I got to that school, somebody had better tell me something, and my son had better been at that school, safe and sound. When I got the call from the director of the school, I dropped everything I was doing to get there. In the back of my mind, I was hoping and praying that this was some bullshit prank they were trying to pull on me 'cause there was no way in the hell Tabatha was that fucking loose in the head that she would lay hands on my son. If I found out she had anything to do with this, on my granny's grave, that bitch was going to meet Jesus.

When I rolled up to the school, my heart sank down to my feet when I saw all the flashing lights. I tried not to let my emotions get the best of me, but with each step I took towards the front office, all logic and reasoning left my mind and was replaced with fueling rage. My skin was burning, and my eyes felt like they'd turned into two balls of fire. If someone didn't let me know what the fuck was going on, I was going to set this entire fucking building on fire.

The second I walked in the building, I saw Secret sitting in a chair next to my mother rocking, bawling her eyes out, which only infuriated me even more. When she looked up and saw me, she ran straight towards me and wrapped her arms around my neck tightly; her entire body was shaking uncontrollably.

"Priest, she took my baby! She has my baby!" She cried out in pain.

"Try to calm down, baby. Let me handle this, aight? Just relax." I sat her back down and redirected my energy to the motherfuckers who were supposed to be in charge of finding my son.

"Somebody got two seconds to tell me what the fuck happened to my son, and how the fuck y'all let that crazy bitch take him."

"Mr. Carter, please calm down. We're doing everything we can."

"No, fuck that! Y'all motherfuckers just sitting around while my son is missing! Don't fucking tell me to calm down! I want to know where my child is right motherfucking now before I flip all shit over!"

"Sir, please try and relax. We're doing everything in our power to bring your son home safely. But you cannot be making idle threats. We're here to help."

"Don't tell me what the fuck to do. Don't tell me to be fucking reasonable when y'all fucking people let this psycho bitch take my son from y'all's care."

"Well, we received an update about thirty minutes ago. The assailant escaped from Emory Health Institute after assaulting and killing one of the nurses during a routine check. We understand that she is your ex-wife, and she was sentenced to serve 120 days of inpatient treatment after attempting to snatch your daughter during a courtroom proceeding."

"Listen to me. I do not give a fuck about none of this bullshit you're talking about right now. I know the bitch that took my son. Where the fuck is she?"

"We haven't had any contact with the assailant since she took off with your son. She was last spotted leaving a gas station about ten miles south of the center. Do you have any idea where she could be going, or why she took your son?"

"If I knew where this bitch was, do you actually think I would be standing right here, lip wrestling with you? All I know is, the bitch crazy and she's capable of doing anything to my kid in order to hurt me or my fiancée. But I will tell you this, y'all better find that bitch before I do."

"Priest, why is she doing this? Why did she take my baby?" Secret's voice snatched my attention away momentarily from the detectives. She was still distraught and shaking like a leaf.

"Look at me, baby," I kneeled before her, cupping her chin to bring her eyes to mine. "I promise you, on my life, I'm bringing my son back home. You hear me? I promise."

"Don't let her hurt my son. Please."

"I'll die first before I let anything happen to him. Trust me, baby. I'm bringing him home."

"What about Aaliyah? Where is she at right now?"

"She's fine. One of the ladies at her school has her safe until we can find Cross."

I tried my best to console Secret without trying to fall apart myself, but it was hard as fuck to hold this shit together. But I knew she needed me to be strong and even if it killed me, I was going to be as strong as I could until my son was safe back with us. While everyone else chatted amongst themselves, trying to pinpoint Tabatha's whereabouts, I did everything I could to contain the anger and fear coursing through my veins. There was no telling what state of mind Tabatha was in when she took my son, and it worried the fuck out of me because I knew how evil and malicious she could be. I just prayed and tried to hold on to my faith that she wouldn't hurt my son because of me.

About twenty minutes had passed and there was still not updates on Tabatha and my son's whereabouts. The only thing I could do was hope that she was holding him hostage as a means to get my attention. As I was scrolling through my phone to see if anyone had posted anything about Tabatha or Cross, a text message from an unknown number came across my phone.

Unknown: **4669 Airport Blvd. Room 120, COME BY YOURSELF!!**

It was nobody but Tabatha's crazy ass, and I could bet my bottom dollar this bitch was going to wish like a motherfucker that this day never fucking happened.

"Mama, take Secret home and stay there until I get back."

"Why? Where are you going?"

"Just do what I ask you to do, please. I'll be back."

I had one thing on my mind as I made my way towards the front door, and that was to choke the life out of this bitch. She wanted to be crazy, but she ain't met a crazy motherfucker until I got ahold of her ass. She may have thought she was waiting to see me, but she was about to get the motherfucking devil.

I skated out of the parking lot in a hurry to the address she'd sent to my phone. It was at a hotel down by the airport, and I wasted no time getting to that room to my son. I didn't know if she was armed or not, but I really didn't give a fuck. I just wanted to lay eyes on my son and see that he was okay. When I made it to room 120, I didn't knock; I tried to kick that bitch in.

"Open this motherfucking door, Tabatha!"

"Are you alone?"

"Open this fucking door right now before I kick this bitch in!" I gave the door another thunderous kick before I heard her clicking the lock to open the door. When I pushed the door open, she was standing back, holding my son in front of her with a knife to his throat. The second he saw me, he tried to run towards me, but she held him back by his collar.

"Daddy?" He called out to me as if he was begging for me to rescue him, and that shit damn near broke me. On everything I love, I swear to God, I was killing Tabatha's ass this day.

"It's cool, Poppa, daddy's here."

"I figured you would come to the rescue for this little motherfucker, but you let the fucking courts take my daughter away from me."

"You did that shit! 'Cause you crazy as fuck. But not as crazy as I'm about to be if you don't take that motherfucking knife from my son's neck, right now."

"Or what? Huh? What are you going to do? I guess he's more important to you than me, huh? Ever since you allowed this little bastard in your life, we've had nothing but troubles, Priest. All I ever wanted was for us to be together, baby. Why did you do this to us? Why did you choose him over me?"

"Tabatha, take the knife off my son. You mad 'cause I hurt you; take that shit out on me. But this is my last time telling you, let my fucking son go."

"Why? So, you can take him and go back to your little family and just leave me all alone? You really think I was just going to let you live this fairytale ass life with that bitch? You got me fucked up, Priest! If I can't have you, this little motherfucker damn sure ain't, and neither will his bitch ass mother."

In that moment, I knew if I didn't act quickly, she would do something to my son. I blacked out and rushed Tabatha, pushing Cross out of the way before connecting a closed fist to her face, dropping her ass to the floor. Throwing the knife out of her reach, I lost all control of myself as I pounded the fuck out of Tabatha's face. Wrapping my hands around her neck, I squeezed until my arms felt like spaghetti noodles, and I knew she was dead. I still didn't let go until I felt Cross tugging at my shirt and calling my name.

"Daddy? Daddy?"

Letting her go, I grabbed ahold of my son and held him close to me. "It's cool, Poppa. Daddy got you, son."

"Bad girl, daddy," he said, pointing at Tabatha's lifeless

body.

"Yeah, she was bad, but the bitch dead now, Poppa."

A Real Happy Ever After

Two Years Later…

"Priest? Priest? It's time to wake up, my boy."

When I opened my eyes, I saw my granny standing next to my bed, smiling down at me. She was dressed in all white with a bright ass glow surrounding her.

"Granny? Damn, I miss you, baby."

"I know you do, baby. But you know I never left you. I'm so proud of you, son."

"I wish you were still here with me, baby."

"I'll always be here, just not physically. Take good care of my great-grandbabies, you hear?"

"I got you, baby. I love you, granny."

"And I love you more, son." Her spirit vanished as the door to my room crept open, and Cross and Aaliyah came running through the door, diving right on top of me.

"Daddy? Daddy? Wake up! It's time to get ready for the party!" Cross yelled in my face.

"It's still early, Poppa. The party ain't till later."

"Uh uh. Mama said you gotta get up now and help her," Aaliyah chimed in.

"Oh, that's what she said? Alright, go tell her I'm coming right now, okay?"

"Okay." They both yelled in unison and took off running

back out of the door.

Sliding out of bed, I went to the bathroom to empty my bladder, brush my teeth, and clean my face. As I made my way downstairs, all I could hear was a bunch of loud noise coming from the family room, and it was like music to my ears. Making my way around the corner in the kitchen, I spotted the most beautiful girl in the world flipping pancakes on the griddle. Easing behind her, I wrapped my arms around her waist and planted a kiss on her cheek.

"Good morning, wife."

"Good morning, husband. It's about time you got up. You know I need your help with these babies."

"I got you, mama. Where my babies at anyway?"

"You don't hear all that loud fuss coming from the family room? They're probably in there raising your mama's blood pressure. The cake and decorations for the party are already at the venue; all you have to do is tame your little ones while I make sure the food and everything is ready."

After all that bullshit with Tabatha, life for me and my family had finally calmed back down. Luckily enough, no charges were brought against me for killing Tabatha, and I was able to finally be done with her forever. I never wanted to hurt her, let alone kill her, but when it came to my kids, I'd blow the world up to protect them. Once the smoke had settled, Secret and I got married on my granny's birthday, like we planned, and several months later, we got the surprise of our lives when we welcomed twins, a girl by the name of Sienna Diamond and a son, Semaj Calvin. Today was their first birthday party, and we planned on going all out. Only this time, we didn't have a delusional ass bitch to ruin another one of my kids' parties.

Celebrating the life of my twins with my wife on my side and my mother being around brought so much joy to my heart; I almost wanted to cry. For a minute, I didn't think I would ever feel this type of love and happiness in my life again, but I was so grateful the good Lord showed a real nigga love and gave me a second chance. Every day, I woke up feeling blessed and honored to call Secret my wife and give her all the love I had inside of me.

"You having fun, daddy?" Secret snuck up behind me, planting a sweet kiss on my lips.

"Of course, I am. And I have you to thank for making all of this possible. I love you so much, Lil' One, and I thank God every day He gave me you as my wife. I can't imagine my life without out, and I thank you for stepping in to be Aaliyah's mom. You take care of her like she's your own and I appreciate that, especially with all the hell we been through."

"She is mine, just like all the rest of them. Thank you for letting me into her life and back into your heart. I love you, husband. And to show you my appreciation, I got a gift for you." She handed me a small gift bag filled with stuffing paper. I could tell by that big ass grin she had on her face, she was definitely up to something.

"What you up to, Lil' One?" I hurriedly pulled the paper out of the bag and found a sonogram picture with the word *Congratulations* written on it.

"What the fuck? Is this real? You pregnant?"

"Six weeks."

"Damn, we on a roll."

"You happy?"

"Am I?" Pulling her close to me, I kissed her lips passionately. "Baby, I'm the happiest I could ever be. I got everything I want and need right here with you. You my lil' Secret. Forever and always."

"And always, we'll be forever."

THE END

(For real this time)

Join Our Mailing List:

http://eepurl.com/gU81k5

9 798842 349432